Log of the S.S.
The Mrs Unguentine

Log of the S.S. The Mrs Unguentine

by Stanley Crawford

WITH A NEW AFTERWORD BY BEN MARCUS

 DALKEY ARCHIVE PRESS CHAMPAIGN AND LONDON

Library of Congress Cataloging-in-Publication Data

Crawford, Stanley G., 1937-
Log of the S.S. The Mrs. Unguentine / Stanley G. Crawford. -- 1st
Dalkey ed.
p. cm.
ISBN 978-1-56478-512-1 (pbk. : acid-free paper)
1. Marriage--Fiction. 2. Diary fiction. I. Title.
PS3553.R295L64 2008
813'.54--dc22
                    2008014615

Partially funded by a grant from the Illinois Arts Council,
a state agency, and by the University of Illinois
at Urbana-Champaign

www.dalkeyarchive.com

Printed on permanent/durable acid-free paper
and bound in the United States of America

For Rosemary

*Log of the S.S.
The Mrs Unguentine*

I

The name is Mrs Unguentine. I was not the one born with it, he was. We were married by telephone when the great cable was laid across the ocean floor well before the weather turned so foul; it was the thing to do then, the thing to do indeed. Some high priest on a party line made us man and wife or at least did consecrate the phone line, the electrodes, or whatever. And made me drop all my names, maiden, first and middle, the result being Mrs Unguentine.

II

Forty years ago I first linked up with
Unguentine and we made love on twin-hulled catamarans, sails a-billow, bless the seas, but Unguentine—now dead after a bloody eventless life—turned out to be a ferocious bastard who beat me within an inch of my life everywhere we sighted land, not because of me, not for land, but for drink, he with his bent for alcohol up to the very last moment when his grey lips touched the blue sea for the final time, moment of his death. Suicide. So I sailed that ship, I sailed it every nautical inch of our marriage.

III

What's worse, as he went overboard,
bottle clutched to his lips and probably already dead of a
rotten liver as he toppled into the froth, what did I see
in his hip pocket? The pocket that concealed a flabby
backside? What did I see? All our navigation charts rolled
up, and so down they went with him to the bottom and
there I was, left alone in the middle of a nasty squall far
from all land. He beat me one last time before he died,
though limply. I should have known. Not a scrap of
land in sight. And now I wonder why I even bother,
this three-thousand-and-no-doubt-somethingth-time it
must be, with Unguentine, ferocious bastard, catamaran,
alcohol, beating, blessed seas, suicide, the sails, the
how and the where, for why multiply anything any
more and heap it all higher, heap and clog?

IV

Yet the thought for example that the miseries of my life with Unguentine might have been brought on by myself as in catamaran, lonely seas, wife, the first and fatal swig at the bottle, and so on. Yelling at him across the wind as he leaned against the tiller, pipe or cigar or baby's rattle clenched between his teeth, for all he wanted was the sea and the depths while I cried for company, my old and dear and so long-lost friends, while I poured him another drink and he drank himself into visions of forever setting sail across oceans unbefouled by man and where women knitted sails or nets or clothes, and sang, not talked, sang with the wind and with the slicing of prows through aqua glazes. Unguentine was a man who grew nauseous upon land, he could not walk upon a solid, unmoving surface without trembling at the thought it might all crack and crumble into bits and drop into some great hole with the dust of beaten mattresses. His terrestrial asthma. And no wonder, for what was then called land, that shambles, was a sorry surface unfit for the conduct of anything but a harrowing traffic. But I kept him on land,

I forced him to skip rope. He did. Our last vessel was a barge, a barge such as is used to tow garbage out to sea with. It was the only way I would go to sea again, I said. We got the thing for a song, garbage and all, rot, stink and a flock of squabbling seagulls. We had the garbage covered with earth and planted trees and flowers, and there was a great canvas with brass fittings to cover it all up from the wind and the waves, and thus we set sail upon a course that kept us to temperate zones, for the sake of my plants. And many times we were halted by hostile navies who had never seen such a sight; once we were claimed by an impoverished government which sought an island cheap by virtue of confiscation. While I watered my plants, Unguentine drank. On some equator or other I added dogs and a cat who ate fish and provided fecal matter for my garden which came to flourish to such a degree that it grew impenetrable in places, while vine-reinforced leafy boughs overhung virtually the whole barge and we could go for days on end without seeing each other, amused at our respective ends by visitations of uncanny birds. I deceived myself into thinking he was happy. Was it not, after all, the year he cracked the Joke? And that was even the year he said he'd rather not do much talking. I had the cat and the dogs, remember. I was not listening very attentively. His unfortunate end therefore took me by surprise two days later, and right after the plunge— the same, bottle, grey lips, frothy seas—immediately after his plunge I rushed to the pilot-house in the interests of keeping the barge on a true course despite my grief and against the possibility of some scuttling going on. I had never visited the pilot-house before. My surprise and shock can then be imagined when I flung open the door and stumbled inside and grasped the pilot wheel and peered through the windows ahead or aft or fore or whatever, forever confused by those silly nautical terms and hating the hairy men who used them, smirking. But of course nothing was visible through the windows but the thick vegetation of the garden, that is, Unguentine had been steering all these years with no idea of what he was steering towards; and as I was now. The motto of his death was simple, as inscribed on a business card tucked between the glass and frame of the window before the pilot wheel: 'Fundamental Ship and Boat Repairs Performed.' That would be his touch, Unguentine's touch, deliberate, thoughtful, and devastating. I knew it. He would have saved that business card from years before for precisely that moment. Our barge most certainly needed no repairs, however. Not one.

V

Unguentine, suicide, the business card,
the barge, alcoholic's leap into the sea, bottle, grey lips,
boughs dragging in sea currents. So goes the sequence,
the awful chain, and between my despair at not knowing how many times I have told it and whether I shall
ever finish telling it once well and decently, I do wonder about that business card, Fundamental Ship and
Boat Repairs Performed, and what if in fact it had
nothing to do with his death? Coincidence? The business card inserted into that gummy little gap between
the glass and varnished wood frame of the pilot-house
window on our ocean-going barge, inserted there casually in the summery sub-equatorial January eleven
months before his death, November it was, with no
connection whatsoever? Possible? For if so, then it means
that my Unguentine with his flowing white hair and
yellow beard that ringed his mouth like a cloud in late
afternoon, it means that he left me with no message at
all, no last words, no final touch other than the act of
leaving itself. Can I say he died with no personal touch
at all? Not even no toppling overboard with bottle to lips,

19

navigational charts in hip pocket? Perhaps then there would be no telling what, no watery punctuation to that eventless life of his, no noise, no error; only his silence.

Sometimes when I am weary of seeing things in that flat, three-dimensional manner once so much boasted of, two plus two, and all the rest, there seems no longer to be any precise moment when old Unguentine vanished from my life, it seems rather an almost gradual process that went on over many years and as part of a great rhythm, as if, through some gentle law of nature, his disappearance would be followed by his gradual re-emergence, that he would come back, so on, so forth. And in fact when I dared venture into the pilot-house that day I knew he would be gone, I knew my hands upon the pilot wheel would do whatever they had to, that all those carelessly listened to remarks about charts and stars and buoys and lighthouses, anchors, piers, waves, swells and so on, all would fall into place, and there I would be confidently sailing our barge towards the luminous brown clouds of some foul but splendid city, there to be forever free of those wanderings. But as I say, there were no navigational charts to be found anywhere on the barge, which is why I assume he took them with him if in fact he had ever used such aids to sail with at all—though here I suppose that if one is to sail anywhere out of sight of land one must carry maps and charts. The point being, since there were no charts, at least I could spare the garden which completely obstructed the view from the pilot-house and made any sort of steering impossible—and here it strikes me that, in practically unbearable truth, my first response to the discovery of Unguentine's death was to cut down the garden. And so I must ask now, so many years later, so far distant from the scene, whose garden? Here, the loveful mourning that casts the prized possessions of the dead upon the pyre? Here, in glee at last the garden unprotected? Whack? Whack?

The former. For the garden on our barge was none other than the famed Unguentine Gardens which have been watered in celebration by the fireboats of all the ports of call that have them, for more than thirty years. How have I presumed to call the gardens ever mine, the great Unguentine Gardens, *cherchez la femme?* True, I have known jealousy. I have watched the gardens grow from tiny seedlings and limp cuttings into cantilevered banks of blossoms of a brilliance such that ocean liners have deflected painstaking schedules to angle for a closer look, and applaud a fragrance a mile off; and trees that have won prizes from councils of men accustomed to viewing nothing less mobile than dashing horses and thundering elephants, in that blood-clogged conspiracy of mammals I used to hear so much about those days. The great Unguentine Gardens, yes, who has not heard of them in their heyday of long ago when the weather was so much better than now, and now when the gardens are fallen and gone, gone in that manner too which time will prevent me from telling their story, piddling story; things grow, things die, is it. And it was Unguentine who planted the trees, forty years ago, in my flower garden on the barge at a particularly sunny latitude, in his quiet manner, before breakfast, at that dawn time when most of us are checking out our joints and searching over our bodies for the lesions and abrasions we are convinced a malign sleep has inflicted upon us, just like that, snap of the fingers, he planted a score of saplings between starting up the powerful steam-engine and weighing anchor, mending even a hole in the standard. He could be a fast worker. And did they ever grow, his trees, under the subtle guidance of brilliant feats of navigation that in the space of a year sought out four springs, four summers, four autumns, four winters, in over sixteen seas and oceans and bays and inlets north and south, in such manner that his trees grew four times faster than what was going on on land, as our barge traced upon the map a course to be envied by a winged insect in its witty feints and dodges amid swallows. Their trunks, stout and plump and shapely, in that way that comes only through sea-going cultivation; their leaves, tinted with variegated greens, spangled and iridescent, marks of their out-landish vintage through springs and autumns of a multitude of latitudes. But where his trees flourished upwards in an orderly manner, sprouting leaves, then letting them go, things were not so easy with me and my flowers, not nearly as hardy against the incessant changes of climate. For months on end I was up all night. One can imagine. Some of the more delicate varieties I had been cultivating for years would bud, bloom and blow in less than an hour and a half, in crises of photo-synthesis as we passed from precipitous springs into sudden summers, temperatures into the hundreds even at midnight. With rake and hoe and pruning shears I would scurry about to pull up wilted flowers one minute, plant more the next, and rush back and forth to my enormous compost heap, seeming end-product of all that frenetic generation and watered with my tears, my sweat, with my arms flailing away at the swarms of foreign bugs often so thick that even seagulls kept their distance, until dawn and beyond, until I might wake up to find myself blundering around our barge-garden carrying a flashlight at high noon, tool of some last night's emergency of pollination.

I saw little of Unguentine. Forever in the pilot-house steering with sextant and calendar, marking off the days not with Xs but with question marks, measuring the height of his growing trees by triangulation, for he never had time to visit the gardens any more. Trees, trees, I could have cut them all down, or poured motor oil on their roots, or let the burning leaves of autumn some-where flame too high. Often he vanished for days down the spiral staircase into the engine-room to overhaul the weary machinery, leaving me with a curt note tacked to his then-favourite aspen, the Aspen Laura-Anne, a white-limbed thing with noisy leaves: 'A due-south drift, please, love, for a day or two, n'est-ce pas?' And I was loyal, I was obedient, my asters be damned. When would it all end? Four–five years this went on. We fuelled by night in obscure, foetid ports where I strip-teased on the prow, ringed by candles, to mollify thin-lipped customs officials, while Unguentine whispered assigna-tions for contraband into the lapping darkness over the stern; one week it was a case of crown jewels, another a cargo of slave babies who sang sweet songs in the depths of the hold while I leaned against partitions and wept, childless, penniless; another time, bananas. The seas, the seas, how I hated them then, and all their waters which glided us from chicanery to chicanery and in our wake, our youth, oil smears iridescent of all that might have been; but never was, never will be. Instead, we threw a great tent up over the barge, over the tops of the young trees, and conducted nautical orgies in tropi-cal seas for bevies of wealthy yachtsmen who traded

23

griping paramours before our very eyes, our open palms and ten per cent, and who would scramble up the tree-trunks to drape themselves nude from limbs, jeering down, and everything would be the noise of boughs cracking and leaves being stripped from twigs, nights of it, years of it. Unguentine drank; my fury went into tossing huge salads. The yachts, the gleaming motor launches, the sloops, the tern schooners with crews of twenty, they ringed our barge like ants feeding from a fat aphid day and night. We were known, we were infamous the world over, as the S.S. *The Mrs Unguentine*, floating fleshpot, ocean-going brothel, were attributed legends, miraculous powers and bumper opium crops, all lies; and how I cursed Unguentine for dragging my name, my only now, through the mud of land and scum.

The barge, poor barge. My flower beds, nightly trampled, dwindled to frightened, dusty clumps such as cower alongside thundering highways of summer, Unguentine's trees to bare-branched skeletons crowned with only a fringe of green, trunks protruding starkly from earth packed solid by the patter of bare feet, and squeals, the heavy breathing, rolling bodies, night after night. I, the sad little figure, aproned and of shy eyes, who filled glasses and broadcast hors d'oeuvres, bottom nightly blued by palpitations of admirals and insipid pinches of millionaires. These were not the people I longed for, these were not my silken people of the past with their soft-spoken voices and elegant poses, grace-fully tweaking the stems of fluted glasses; they were vandals all, and we a colonial island befouled and ravished by each passing ship. Once we were pursued by a floating casino jealous of our attractions, she ran aground on a reef our barge slid clanking over, though

24

dropping propellor and rudder. Unguentine as ever improvised and on we sailed to other careers, *The Mrs Unguentine* retiring hastily from service in one port only to be re-launched, with paint-job and fanfare, in some other, as ocean-going rest home with international cuisine and daily sea-burials; as the last and briefly rented stand of a government in exile, that sea-sick king, his neurasthenic queen; as Les Bazaars Unguentine with high-class optical goods, duty-free and one third off; as, armed with three cannon, shrouded in the blanched guise of a canvas iceberg, nocturnal guano pirate. We made, stole, frittered millions in currencies hard and soft, courted the brink of disaster for years on end, lived in constant terror through a time of endless navigational blunders which, Unguentine claimed, were brought on by our heavy load of vegetables and plants, and sudden shifts in the climatic zones which rendered useless his maps, ambushing us with incredible situations. 'You fool,' I dared to say that time he sailed us plumb into an arctic sea right in midwinter and we ran aground on a submerged island of ice whose heavings and bucklings thrust the hull of the barge high up into the air until the whole thing keeled over, with a long and bitter winter spent on ice, the thirty-degree tilt at which we did everything, ate, slept, crawled, saving the gardens only by means of hastily constructed earthworks and terraces, tree props, guy wires, heated and gassed by home-made smudge pots. Once in attempting to outrun a high and vicious tidal wave, our top speed proved inadequate and we were swept up and borne along by it, surfed at high speed half a day or more, Unguentine at the pilot wheel with eyes closed and teeth clenched and steering straight ahead, while below deck I manned

the pumps against spraying leaks of the ancient iron hull;
the wind ripped out half the trees and sucked away all
our chickens except the rooster, leaving us three months
without a supply of fresh brown eggs, extra large.
Plagues of insects we have known, chattering hordes
came out of the middle of the night to munch their way
across half the garden by dawn and multiply faster than
we could shoo them away; and heavy night-flying sea-
birds which have crashed by the flock into the trees as I
have wandered about the barge by candlelight, the dull
thuds and cracking limbs, the hiss of leaves being
sheared from branches, and my arms thrashing about,
my body socked and cannonaded clear across the lawn
by those feathered carcasses.

But there came calmer seas, we came to know even
bouts of respectability and glory in the Unguentine
Gardens years when, refurbished, replanted, we bobbed
in leisure from port to port, the paid admissions, the
aquatic parades, the holding of high-minded botanical
banquets and ecological conferences, all in the days
when things like that could still be done. We flew the
flag of a diseased republic anxious for mail-order reve-
nue, a pretty thing depicting the Milky Way upon a
field of blue, and huge, nine by twelve, entirely hand-
blocked by starving peons whose government com-
memorated the registration of our barge by inventing the
sweet-flowing River Unguentine; and who cared that it
was only a flood-control channel, for it was fame and a
mark, geography with all the pomp of speakers' plat-
forms and waving banners and idle crowds, who cared
but Unguentine? Who saved the barge then? Who suddenly noticed his disappearance only minutes before he
was scheduled to unveil the bronze plaque? I did. I

26

scurried below deck, by luck. There he was, hoisting a jackhammer into position to have a fatal go at the bottom. 'Don't do that,' I said. Thus we made it on to the map and a million multi-coloured postage stamps, though so briefly.

Little else do I remember of those fifteen–twenty years besides the sound of the waves, and seagulls, the engine, the interminable squawking of Unguentine's all-band portable radio as he listened to weather reports in the fourteen languages he had mastered expressly for that purpose, a snatch of each, while I had only two with which to chatter myself from madness to madness, now dwindled to the tatters of one. I saw little of him then, or saw him mainly at a distance. But then one day he summoned me, it was a summer day of crystal-line air that made the horizon meeting of sea and sky into a fold, a seam, an overlapping, a wire, anything, and I hung lazily about the railings, sometimes dabbing at them with paint, longing overboard for land and people, he summoned me in his manner, which was to leave a note in the path he knew would soon be mine. As I said, I was dabbing at the railings with a paint-brush. My ear pricked up when suddenly, working away at the underside of a T-joint, the hairs of my brush touched off a scratchy resonance. I leaned over. And there, now covered with the bright sienna of anti-rust paint, was a small square of paper taped to the under-side of the railing pipe. I ripped it off, carefully wiped away the paint. 'Darling, do be at the lawn at noon, eh?' it said, the lawn being a small plot of grass in the very center of the barge and surrounded by Unguentine's trees in such a way that we could have a spot of rural privacy even amid the commerce of a great port. I had not seen him for days though knew he was somewhere around, what with the notes, the way we moved across the ocean by fits and starts, the steam-engine sometimes running at full speed and the wind rushing through the trees, at others adrift in a practically dead calm, I knew he was still there, somewhere. Not that I wanted to see him. His summoning me no doubt meant he had some project in mind for me and I dreaded to think what, lunch, dinner, afternoon tea. So I lolled about on the lawn and waited, for who could know what noon meant in the kind of lives we led. The sunlight flickered brightly into the depths of branches. He had planted evergreens around this little lawn, pines, fir, a redwood, some cedars, and already within so few years the spot was sunny only near noon on the equator; that particular day it was over a hundred degrees and hidden sprinklers sprayed a fine and cooling mist all over the barge: from a distance, it was said, often we were seen as a greenish cloud, a tuberous mirage, a ship of war. I waited. The grass beneath my feet ceased quivering as the steam-engine fell silent. Moments later something thrashed about behind the screen of evergreens. A branch cracked. Being the wife of Unguentine called for nerves of steel at times. Then silence. I was to speak only if and only when spoken to. The brush of pine needles against a hollow, metallic surface. Then, heavy, rhythmic breathing.

He declared a time of rest, twenty minutes, or so I thought he said with that especially fleshly tongue of his which prevented him from speaking distinctly and rapidly, his mouth so full of it few words ever squeezed out, that iguana-like tongue weight, so gagging. I smiled. Thus we ambled about the barge, arm in arm.

Unguentine had grown his trees in such a way that, now in their early maturity, they were capable of generating their own little climates about them no matter which way we sailed, no matter where the sun was, or moon, or what rains, the northerly side of the barge remaining so throughout all twirls of the compass and seasons beyond the decks; further, he was thus able to keep four seasons on board, in balance, moving them fore to aft, or whatever, four times a year, like swarms of bees; though we never had snow. Thus we wandered about the decks, now hot, now cold, until we reached the pilot-house where we fell to making love amid the greasy fixtures of a dismantled auxiliary generator, my eyes, my weeping eyes tracing the dark lines of that rough wood floor across the sill and beyond deck to the mirror-sheen of surface of whichever ocean we now lay upon, on a morning no mists had risen to fuzz the horizon, no mirages. Unguentine lowered the skiff and rowed us out past the fat, drooping chain of the barge's anchor, a few hundred yards out, where we held a picnic. We embraced again. I was crying. I could hear Unguentine's deep voice grunting something into my hair. An explosion rang out. This, I thought, could be anything. But before I knew what was happening, champagne was coursing down my throat, I was laughing, scarcely following the line sighted by his index finger, black with grease, towards our barge, his thickly murmured word: 'Rainbow.' How could I see through my tears? A breeze billowed over us. Then Unguentine lowered the oars. With a grace that meant to draw the surface of the water beneath us, he bent his naked back and swung his arms to and fro, soundless, and so we returned. I was still sobbing when he lifted me aboard,

29

imprinting my body with his greasy fingerprints. That was the first time I had been off it for two years. Two years. By any calculation.

VI

At the sound of the splash I sprang to the
rail, peered overboard. I had not been far off. Bending
over a flower bed, weeding. Sweeping a deck. Such
things. And now I stared down into the foam of his
white splash sliding over the wound in the sea like the
knitted fingers of the elderly. Then bubbles, his last
globes of carbon dioxide. Free at last? So I thought, and
would soon have dashed to the pilot-house to set sail on
a course due-north for some great harbor where I might
sell the barge for a handsome price, to live out my life
on land, my days; parched throat, sea legs to the end.
Years and years. Packages one unwraps, then wraps up,
again unwraps, brown paper, twine, excelsior, an un-
wanted gift. But I was wrong. Suddenly out of the
turquoise depths a shiny form wiggled surfacewards and
shot into the air like a jumping trout, to splash back. A
gaff was handy; I netted it. Inside, a note: 'Will be back
in an hour or so.' Of course. As was sometimes his
wont this time of morning, he'd gone for a plunge in his
hand-made diving bell, a thing of beaten brass and
capable of extraordinary depths. So I went back to what

I had been doing. Swept a deck. Bent over a flower bed, weeded. Such things. Humming a resigned tune. For such were the days when Unguentine's forty trees were grown stout and healthy enough that we could sail anywhere in the world so long as we avoided arctic ices and equatorial heats. My work was simple and fulfilling, but hard. I watered and trimmed the flower banks, raked up the leaves under the trees, gathered fallen branches to dry out on the bow for firewood, I tended the vegetable garden we had growing in a small plot aft of the lawn and which was richly fertilized by ground-up seaweed, I fished, I cooked when we tired of raw food; I mended the ancient clothes we rarely had occasion to wear; and mushrooms I grew on trays in the bilge next to the chicken coop. We had ducks, too, mallards with clipped wings; they kept down the snails. One cat, two dogs, retired port mongrels. Also a goat. From twin vines that formed a natural awning over the stern pilot-house deck, we yearly harvested grapes, pressed them, casked and drank the wine whenever we sensed from over the horizon, on a distant land, an aura of national celebration. Cheers to some people (I would murmur, our glasses colliding), some race, as they commemorate some fine hour within the sadness of history.

Unguentine was about and visible more than ever before, his darkly tanned body now striding the length of the barge to fetch a hammer and wrench—as I might press myself against a bulkhead to clear a path—now crouching on the deck wet from my waterings to secure a length of rope, lubricate a winch, assemble his latest device. Long hours he spent in the uppermost branches of the tallest tree, the fast-growing Cottonwood Elizabeth, gangly thing, with field-glasses pointed out to sea,

looking over the driftwood and floating debris with
which he made up the machinery of our lives, and the
ships, the countless ships which often cluttered our
route and menaced our navigations, and abandoned all
as if sailing the seas had gone out of fashion. Indeed,
no wonder, with those waves, those swells. Whenever
the weather was windless and calm, Unguentine would
take the skiff and row out to sea, and soon the horizons
would ring and chatter under the distant detonations of
the charges with which he cleansed the seas of ships
and floating wrecks, sending up plumed geysers as they
went down, gasping, gulping in a last indigestible drink.
Single-handedly he scuttled the fleet of a great nation,
taking weeks to do it; and on the decks of one tall ship
he found laid out the numbered stone blocks of an
historic monument which I thought I remembered seeing
as a child, having eaten roasted chestnuts in its presence;
if that childhood was ever mine and all that seemed to
follow. From the bow half of an abandoned freighter
probably broken up in a hurricane, and one of the last
ships we were ever to see, he salvaged the materials for
a towering salt-water distillation plant which he installed
on the south side of the pilot-house with some of its
solar panels hanging over the rudder, eastwards, in a
most unsightly manner. But we had no choice, for the
barge, grown heavy and cumbersome under its weight
of vegetation, could no longer be so speedily navigated
in and out of rain zones. Many times for days on end
we floated through the dismal wreckage of aircraft
disasters, the split-open suitcases, the dead, the limbs,
the only other people we were ever then to see, and
with a net between prayers we fished up a fine set of
silverware, an alarm clock, a kerosene lantern, several

volumes of an encyclopedia. One day, inexplicably, for the sea was like that, we came across a sturdy raft bearing a flawlessly new electric stove, refugee of some inland flood or advertisement, and Unguentine stripped it down to pieces small enough to fit through the hatchway and down the stairs to my galley where he hooked it up; the raft we took in tow as a swimming platform. Likewise we acquired deck-chairs, sofas, bedding, linen, teacups, curtains.

The barge being ancient but without history, built in the olden days of sound hulls, Unguentine was all the time repairing its fixtures decrepit with over-use, the steam-engine whose bearings always over-heated, the cracked propeller shaft whose wooden splints flew off at regular intervals, the rudder which jammed only in calm seas and usually late in the afternoon. He would emerge from the engine-room covered in black grease except for the red patches of blood where he had nicked and scraped himself on hands and feet, and his flowing white beard protected with a bandana, but with a smile visible: he had done it again, repaired some crucial part with only a slight loss of speed. The engine-room could be a cozy place in the middle of whatever winter we might have happened to choose in an escape from an excess of summer, the warmest spot when the galley stove was off, where we could huddle alongside the tall and gleaming steam-engine, arms entwined, swaying back and forth to its syncopations, its throbbings, sighs, groans, squeaks, hisses, all night, until a cloudy dawn. Then with a yawn, above deck. Calisthenics in the fog. The long day's work forever expanding the gardens, covering every inch of deck and roof with pots of shrubs and flowers, with the barrels, cans and buckets salvaged from sea-currents, with soil we composted and mulched ourselves, watered with our own water distilled from the sea. Unguentine was happy; I was radiant. I adopted at times his method of communication by notes, though to the bolus of paper spurting from the bathroom tap, to the lamination suddenly unyielding to teeth and tongue while eating a sandwich, I would always reply in my manner, directly, to the point, with only a moderate delay, by leaving a note tacked to the pilot-house door in plain view. He never seemed affronted by that, at least. One such dialogue took four days to complete. My glowing message: 'I never want to see land again!!' Time passed, dawns and dusks. At last his reply: 'You never will, my dear.'

I didn't know what to think. At first it seemed he might be answering one of my earlier messages, but of those I could remember none fitted the reply. Or he was simply wrong. I knew there must be land nearby; with his navigations, I knew he must be flirting with coasts just beyond the line of sight. Had not a flock of heavy land-birds descended upon our greenery suddenly one midnight, refusing to depart except under a full blast of our sprinkler system? They left behind some broken branches, white stains, innumerable red feathers, a speckled egg or two. Casually I spied on Unguentine as he pored over his maps and charts in the pilot-house, but saw nothing unusual in his addition of a reef here, his erasure of a strand there, the shift of an island a degree this way or that, corresponding no doubt to the kneading and agitating action of the sea. There were times I swore to hear the throb of the motors of a distant ship, the rush of a jet plane like a sheet being torn in half, times when I knew Unguentine had nothing to do with these sounds, for he was in the habit of amusing me, or so he hoped, by imitating all manner of urban noises, the traffic of cars, buses, trains, distant sirens and bells, the patter of footsteps on a crowded street, carnivals, pounding surf, applause, the swarming murmur of some genteel gathering. He could drive me to tears doing that, standing on a ladder and pruning a limb, his back towards me, blowing all those noises out of his mouth. I could tell it was him. His whiskers always quivered. 'Will you shut up?' I'd shriek from the far end of the barge. Glad therefore I was when he took to spending whole days towards the bottom of the sea in that diving-bell of his, and I was left alone, could rush upstairs from the galley as many times as I wanted to, to see what sound that was. But there was nothing to see, nothing but the rafts of seeming trash Unguentine was bringing up from below. Fat timbers and beams of some heavy, sea-soaked wood. Packing-crates as tall as a man and sealed with barnacles. Barrels and barrels of angular fixtures made of some once-fashionable metal. Coils of cable, rope. Nuts. Bolts. Screws. For days this went on. The polished diving-bell, glowing like the sun, bursting up through the waves, and Unguentine flinging open the hatch and hauling in by hand and by winch ropes to which were attached, floated and pontooned, his latest finds, soon breaking surface and shedding sea-waters; then he would lash it all to the side of the barge, go under again. At night, weary and sopping wet, he would clamber stiffly on board with a basket of deep-sea clams tucked under his arm, bolt down his dinner, fall asleep at the pilot wheel.

When Unguentine had collected enough odds and ends to make our barge resemble one of those protected corners of a beach, or a cove, where the sea-currents

unload all their trash and run, construction began. He
hewed, planed, sawed, mitred the sea-seasoned lengths
of hickory and ash and oak into an astounding series of
struts, no two alike, which, one moonlit night while I
was in bed with a fever, he slung over the barge in the
form of a great dome, well over three stories high and
clearing even the tops of the tallest of his forty trees,
then Elizabeth and the Poplar Agnes. I awoke, staggered
from my bed at dawn to see him way up there on the top
of this spider's web of a thing, pounding in the last and
topmost wooden peg, sledge-hammer raised high over his
head, his bare toes scarcely gripping the wide-spanned
struts, so high in the sky. Keystone to what now? I sighed.
Shall we all be covered with canvas and no longer even
see the sea? The sky? Cooling winds? Hot breezes? Gone
forever too? No, thank God. Soon with crowbar and
hammer he was prying open the packing-crates and
sliding out sheets of high-impact glass made in some city
I once loved; he cut and trimmed them, laid and puttied
them into their casements which opened and closed like
wings all over the dome, then spent days rigging the
windows up, hundreds in all, to a system of ropes and
pulleys and counterweights by which each and every
pane might be opened to any degree by turning a crank
in the pilot-house, with only one hand. Thus the light
remained with us, the breezes, but a sunlight now
refracted by crystalline glass, faintly watery, aquatic,
with subtle auras, and inside the dome as the light grew
dim towards the end of the day, all my flowers would
multiply in mirror in the sky, stars suddenly come near
to ring the image of my little face up there, staring rapt
and wondrous as all the windows slowly tilted and
sealed shut; into night and our silent, dark aquarium.

My work increased with the dome, for there were windows to wash inside and out, their opening angles to be adjusted according to current light, temperature and humidity readings four times daily when it was summer outside, twice when winter, but my happiness was such that I could not complain; indeed, there was no time. And my joy at seeing Unguentine so content. A smile, I knew, was fixed beneath his fine-spun beard which concealed his mouth like a yellow window-shade. He no longer had to worry about those fierce winds which could blow down the whole of his stand of trees in a single gust, the labour of propping them back up one by one, the nursing of their torn roots with vitamins, limbing the shattered branches. Now in the secrecy before dawn he would mount the scaffolding and paste a little note of encouragement to the glass, way up high, sometimes on the inside of the panes, sometimes outside, often cleverly both, and I would scrape them off. Later in the morning as I might be polishing the last and uppermost of the panes outside, he would scramble up the side with the aid of a rope—often leaving footprints on my freshly cleaned glass—and stretch out on top of the dome and doze in the sun, binoculars rising and falling on his bare belly. Then I would join him and we would take turns scanning the sea for floating bottles. Our forty years' voyage yielded perhaps twenty-five found in this manner. The best days being overcast and greyish with the horizon distinctly etched, a sea so flat and calm that each ripple would seem to have its own character. Then the telltale green or blue glint. Unguentine would pass me the field-glasses and slide down the side of the dome, his bare feet striking the deck with an awful whack. To my shouts he would navigate towards the speck. News at last, I chanted, news at last! I remember the day. I never learned. The barge was now drifting. The gap but a hundred yards. Unbelieving, I slid down to the deck. This was no ordinary bottle we were drawing near to, no simple wine bottle, but a huge blue thing of five gallons riding high on the waves and crammed with papers. Unguentine emerged from the pilot-house and lowered himself into a prone position on the deck with his dark hair-matted arm reaching through the railing, fingers dipping into the water, the hissing and bubbling of the steam-engine boiler coming from a porthole open nearby and seeming to fill the whole black sky, while I held his other hand between my two, my feet planted firmly on deck. I saw his fingers stretch wide as we drifted closer. His breathing tight, whistling through his nose. Strands of his long white hair trailed in the water. Then the tips of his fingers touched the bottle and spun it closer. He grasped its neck. I shouted. But that was that. As usual he flung his shirt or some cloth over the thing and hurried away with it to a hiding-place I never discovered. Perhaps he muttered something about it not being fit for a woman to read, later in the day, noting the despondent cast in my eyes. It could have been anything. To the very end he was to forbid me all reading matter other than what was already on the barge, encyclopedias, dictionaries, repair manuals, cookbooks, agricultural publications. Everything I needed ever to know was in there, he once tried to tell me. Still, I squeezed some consolation from those bottles we hit upon every year or so, in knowing there was at least some news about even though I might never see it.

We stayed at anchor that day for the spring seeding, planting and grafting, and opened the dome windows

wide to admit passing flocks of insect-eating birds, and
the trees chattered happily as they went about their
work. Unguentine discouraged overnight stays and
nesting, however, and towards sunset he would go
about the barge with a long pole and gently beat the
branches until the little grey birds would fly away with
a pathetic twig clutched in the bill and no doubt suffer-
ing under the illusion that there would be another barge
such as ours within easy flying distance where they
could rest in peace. Unguentine's attitude being that we
could not afford to feed them continuously; also we had
a few pair of doves and pigeons. I was always saddened
to see those flocks flutter through the windows and
circle the barge a time or two before setting off in the
dusk, a handful of peppercorns cast to the winds, and
would have to rush down to the antechamber off the
engine-room that was our bedroom to weep for the
children I would never have, that being before I had the
courage to do so in front of him. There I would lie in
wait for him to note my absence. He would, in three or
four hours. Finally when he climbed below deck after
dark, wondering where his dinner was, perhaps with
a storm come up and rough seas and blinding rains, I'd
sulk and lure him into the warm and steamy darkness
and from the hairs of his warm body I'd breed a myriad
smiling, sparkle-eyed one-year-olds, my broods, my
flocks. In the churning seas, below the waves, together
inside our hammock woven in coarse sailcloth by Unguentine's deft hands, a spherical webbed sack which
hung and swivelled between the two walls of our bedroom, we would spin round and round with lapping
tongues and the soft suction of lips, whirling, our
amorous centrifuge, all night long, zipped inside against

40

the elements. Now, years and years later, those nights, the thought and touch of them is enough to make me throw myself down on the ground and roll in the dust like a hen nibbled by mites, generating clouds, stars and all the rest.

VII

When was that morning I was out on
the stern deck hanging up the wash on the line that ran
from the distillation plant to the flagpole and back,
thinking it no doubt not long enough to hold the huge
basketful at my feet? When? Lost in futile reveries of far
lands and times which seemed then more and more like
erroneous transmissions from other lives, not mine, not
of my time; and more so now. No matter when. All I
know, it had been a long and exhausting decade. A wind
had come up, a fitful thing that blew hard and then
suddenly dropped, and there I was grappling with wet
laundry as it flopped about and would not stay pinned
to the line, and wondering what would blow off first into
the sea, overalls, underwear, socks, or the whole line. I
was bending over the basket when to my back a gust of
wind blew open the stern door with a clatter. From
inside the pilot-house there came a panicked shout from
Unguentine. I raised my head. Drifting out of the door-
way and tossed and turned up over my head by the
wind, there sailed a large sheet of paper. In the nick of
time I stretched to tiptoes and plucked it from the air.

There were inscriptions, marks. I smoothed it out against a bulkhead. It was one of Unguentine's maps. I had never looked so close up at one before. Fascinated, I let my eyes swim all over the bright mass of colour which depicted some hemisphere or other and which was scribbled with indications of sea-currents and trade winds and storm centers and mean annual temperatures, reefs, shoals, shallows. From the long hours I had seen him poring over them, I gathered that he was reworking them for precision and accuracy. A nice piece of drafts-manship, I thought. Some suitable, mellow hour, I would remind myself to compliment him. Then I realized there was something different about this map, something missing: it was land. There was not a scrap of land anywhere on it. Utterly bald. I gaped. Only water over all this quarter or half a globe? What? How? But soon he was at my side humming. Gently teasing the paper from my wet fingers. I let it go. The slam of the stern pilot-house door as he went back inside. So that was the way things were, I thought, and set about walking up and down the narrow walkways of the barge, snapping off a sprig of mint to press to my nose, pausing now and then before the long lists of nautical terms Unguentine had posted here and there for my instruction, in his concern that I use the right vocabulary while at sea. I memorized the lists, but to no effect. I had no one to talk to. Unguentine's notes were terse, less than a dozen words each. It had been years since we had sighted another ship whole and intact, with living people on the decks, and I could no longer climb the dome and hang out great banners proclaiming certain unfortunate aspects of our marriage, inviting relief, rescue, consolation. Once I wrote a long letter to an old friend, tied it to the

44

feet of one of our pigeons which I secretly dispatched in a midnight gale; next day I found Unguentine silently reading the letter in the pilot-house, his only comment being a grunt, the crackling sound of it being folded up, handed back. So I went on with my chores. What else could I do?

Little, for life on our barge was not conducive to much more than just keeping it going, watering the plants and sailing on from climate to climate, and though there were times when I might wish for it all to sink with a muddy gurgle, there were also others, timeless, without cages, with only leaves and blooms and a silent man. From atop the dome whose prisms I daily polished the gardens were beautiful beyond any memory I might some day have of them. In the very center of the barge, Unguentine's forty trees with an inner circle of ever-greens, cool, dark, unchanging, and surrounded by a flowing ring of deciduous trees, the rounded and drooping boughs of sycamores, elms, oaks, horse-chestnuts, a beech with a white trunk, a red maple, a weeping willow and others whose leaves flashed from hue to hue several times a year. Beneath them, ferns and mosses and an assortment of tropical plants accustomed to a sunless housing, with freshwater ponds here and there with lotuses, water-lilies, watercress, cattails, and bright fresh-water fish, descendants of those netted from the mouth of a great tropical river we once sailed across. At night when all was illuminated by the powerful flood-lights Unguentine had salvaged from an abandoned dredge, the dome as seen from inside reflected the gardens in its five hundred panes and faceted and rearranged all the leaves and flowers into patterns of nameless intricacy, kaleidoscopic. Nude we would caper then, eyes domewards, fascinated by the pornography of our disembodiment, as if beneath a leafy heaven and the limbs of lounging gods, as it used to be all painted.

The barge, although sealed in against the elements, was always in need of refurbishment and improvement; we spent countless years towards its perfection. A vast increase in vegetation beneath the dome had ended up generating an acute problem of heat and humidity whose solution turned out to be splendid. The uppermost panes, two hundred in all, Unguentine uncaulked, removed, cleaned and silvered in such a way that a certain percentage of the sun's rays would be deflected. With re-installation, the effect was successful. Also, he stripped down all the wooden casements and struts inside and out with a wire brush, treated the wood, then applied new coatings of a special hybrid lichen he had developed, a bluish growth which rendered the dome structure almost invisible in certain lights. It must have been during those long hours up on the dome, on the bamboo scaffolding, in the blaze of sunlight and atop the empty sea, the almost breezeless air, that he first con-ceived the way to rid ourselves of the steam-engine, whose ghastly fumes would fill up the dome in certain winds and cover all the leaves with soot, and whose ceaseless thumping all hours of the night often set off unnerving vibrations in the dome, angered the bees. Nor was there any hope of replacing the old engine, about to give out on account of the low-grade sea-scavenged fuel Unguentine fed it, and whose stop-gap repairs were consuming more and more of our time. So he set me to work spinning up several bales of fine cotton he'd found one day into a heavy thread which I then wove into three hundred yards of sailcloth on a huge spool; next I cut it into five hundred triangular shapes about two feet each on the hypotenuse, hemmed and shrunk the lot, and thus our sails were ready. Meanwhile, Unguentine rigged up cables all over the inside of the dome by day, and after dark pored over drawings and plans on the galley table in calculation of wind speeds, drag, tensions, weights, control vectors, nautical aesthetics. With block and tackle and hydraulic jacks he laboriously moved the pilot-house astern two yards in order to have a better angle for the master control cable which was to be buried out of sight down the middle of the garden, secondary cables feeding out from it, also buried, like spines on a fishbone. Luck had it that out one day in his diving bell he hit upon a submerged cargo of pulleys, brought up more than the two thousand he needed and most in good condition. A few squeaked; he threw those away. Months passed. He excavated the garden to lay the conduits for the cables, a noisy and urban time with rows of ditches and heaps of raw earth, stacks of tile pipes, and the sea-driven cement mixer endlessly sloshing. The scars in the lawn were to last a year. Then, conduits laid, cables threaded and tested, the garden restored to order, and during a week predicted to be windless and sunny at our particular latitude and longitude, Unguentine mounted the outside of the dome and fastened down and hooked up the five hundred sails each the size of a manly handkerchief, each subtly controlled by the cable system from the pilot-house where he had installed a great lever, hand-carved and amazing, with which the sails might be trimmed at three speeds, Slow, Moderate, Fast.

The success of the sails was so absolute and stunning that Unguentine immediately took apart the old steam-engine and dropped it into the sea, piece by piece. With each sail being the equivalent of one horsepower in a brisk wind, no telling what in a good gale, the barge was now capable of higher speeds in addition to being fumeless and vibration-free and became a far better place to live on, its climate improving markedly and the sailing of it a thing of glorious sensations. In calm weather the sails could be folded out of sight in such a way as not to obstruct the passage of sunlight on its way into the dome to our plants; with sails extended fully, taut and billowing and shimmering, the whole dome would creak and sing in the wind at the sky beyond, concealed behind a white mask which admitted only cracks of blue whose bright crescents played over the trees and flowers in the garden, glowing somberly green under this strange new daylight so much like life be-neath an umbrella at the beach, as a child. Come autumn in some corner of the barge and piles of dead leaves we had no room for composting, Unguentine would trim the north-west sails, open the windows beneath them and all the leaves would whisk away as if sucked out by a great vacuum cleaner. Likewise, rain-showers outside could be directed and concentrated to anywhere within the garden down to an area three by four. At certain latitudes and usually late in the afternoon, the barge would generate spectacular mirages of itself on the horizon, sometimes two and three at a time, upside-down and banana-shaped, countless points of light blinking and neon, gaudy beyond all belief. I saw them often while atop the dome repairing sails, my new job in addition to cleaning the glass, and by far my favourite. When control lines broke, I spliced them back together again. When a sail needed replacing, it was I who

48

fetched a new one from the hamper and scaled the
outer fence of the dome. Many hours I spent up there
alone and singing with the wind. Hanging on to my little
bucket. My squeegee. My sail-mending kit. Replacement
halyards, eyehooks, brass swivels, grommets. The mallet.
The little block of hardwood, souvenir of the Maple
Rowena, felled by blight, against which I pounded with
one hand, the other clutching a strut, a ripped sail
flapping in the wind. The view, when I had time, exhil-
arating and grand. There might even seem, as I would
lift a sail and peep through the glass at the garden three
stories below, the goat grazing at a pile of brush, ducks
waddling from one pond to another, nothing else I could
possibly desire.

However, such was not the case. My anguish concerning certain aspects of our long life together always
struck me most forcefully at the breakfast table. Warm
mornings we would take breakfast to the very end of
the stern deck behind the pilot-house, sometimes sit on
the deck itself, legs dangling overboard, as seagulls
threaded back and forth over our white wake and eyed
our movements, our toast, fried eggs. Or more often we
would throw open the back doors and sit just inside the
dome and gaze out upon the seascape framed by the
wistaria that grew around the distillation plant, and
perhaps in the distance the glinting fins of playful
dolphins. We always rose early and ate just before
sunrise in the mists like mildew on the surface of the
sea, on colourless waters, on waters lightly tinted blue
or pink, sometimes yellow, calm waters flecked here and
there with blue leaves and silver lips where a breeze
would drive a ripple up. Several hundred yards out, that
white line of foam which marked the border between

fresh water and salt, for the vegetation of our barge generated so much fresh water that we were perpetually ringed by a sort of inner tube of it, a lake floating in the sea, over seventy feet deep, and where swam the hundreds of carp-like descendants of goldfish that once lived in our fish-ponds, also minnows, guppies, angelfish, bluegills. At night they would gain the shelter of the tangle of roots of Unguentine's thirty specially grafted aquatic pines that grew out over the decks all around the barge, trunks and boughs cantilevered over the water by cables attached to the dome struts; though those roots, I cursed them often for the way they sprawled all over the decks and down into the water, being hard to sweep around and easily tripped over. Unguentine invariably woke with a frown. It usually lasted through breakfast. The way he raised his lower eyelids so that his eyes seemed to be peeping over walls. His expression thus fixed and while his coffee went cold and toast grew brittle, he would linger over the morning's readings from the meteorological instruments, wind speed, the night's precipitation if any, the behaviour of currents, air and water temperatures, the barometer, cloud-patterns on the horizon as compared to his home-made cloud chart. Now and then he would look up, nibble at a piece of toast, inserting the rest into his slingshot and speeding it through the air far out into the salt water, for those four or five aged sea-fish of his that kept following the barge. Croakers, I believe. During these pauses, I might try to attract his attention. Suddenly whipping out my make-up kit to re-apply my lipstick or correct an eye-shadow. At best he would notice, would knit his fingers into a basket for his chin, thrust his head forward and stare at me blankly while I did my face. I might seize the

50

opportunity to utter a cheerful word or two. Ho! Ho! Such. But from him, no comment. He would lean back in his chair and plunk an elbow on the table, its riot of dirty dishes gleaming in the rising sun, and dab a drop of coffee from his white beard, squinting into the distance. His manner was usually to vanish for the remainder of the day; the skill with which he did this never ceased to startle me. His brusque departures seemed to be timed to the split-second to coincide with the kettle coming to the boil, or with that moment when the table-cloth was billowing away and about to drop into the water, or just as the cat was jumping up on the breakfast table, or at any of the other innumerable instants when a gesture would have to be made, when the reflex machinery could not be stopped, when I was totally absorbed in some brief action. The glass doors would slam with a clatter, and he would be gone. I was not to follow. The squeaky tread of tennis shoes dying in the distance. Or those little noises of his from the pilot-house, his grunts, coughs, the hum, the snapping of fingers.

But year after year, this could not go on. Annually I attempted reforms. My manner was to present him a typed sheet of remarks at breakfast-time, neatly folded on his plate like a napkin: 'I have noticed lately, my dear, these past three to four years you have not opened your mouth to speak literally one word, preferring rather to nod, wave your arms about, and the like, to the point I hardly know who you are any more, not that I ever did. Nor that I complain. Our bliss, I know, has been fantastic. The last crop of pumpkins broke all records for size and tastiness. Our hybrid zinnias have attained blooms nineteen inches in diameter, glow in the dark.

51

We have identified and named three new species of
porpoise. I love that diamond necklace you brought up
last week. Yet these things, however fulfilling they may
be, scarcely add up to tell me what you refuse to speak,
and if you could possibly see fit to spare a moment now
and then to take me into your confidence, discuss
something, anything in fact, then I might venture to
suggest—brazen hypothesis, I know—that we could start
working our way towards the heart of the matter, on the
way to engaging in many a colourful argument, discus-
sion, seminar, so on, so forth. Permit me to cite a few
examples of the things you have never spoken to me of.
Your mother, for one, your no doubt dear old mother.
Then there's your father, your brothers, sisters, assorted
relatives, friends. Then there are countless items about
your own person, your likes and dislikes, past adven-
tures, the scar on your left kneecap. What did you think
of the soup last night? The state of your health? Any
colds lately? A brief sketch is all I would like. An anec-
dote or two. The juicy peccadillo, say. Even blasphemy.
Such facts, trivial even, I would love to hear more of, or
simply of, and would willingly dote on to pass the time
of day and to know somewhat more fully the silent
stranger I now so selflessly serve and not even wondering why any more, that being the way things happen to
have worked out, God knows how. Past experience,
agreed, has been somewhat grim in this connection, that
is, if I remember correctly, or if you do. That's another
thing. For, rare times we did talk, years ago, you would
claim not to remember things I could still see clearly.
And then you'd recall things I scoffed at as improbable,
unlikely, impossible, and when we did both agree on
something, it usually had nothing at all to do with either

of us. The colour of the sea in a certain morning light
seven and a half years prior. A dense and clammy fog
that stayed with us nine days. So on. So that where I
once did not know who or what you were, now I wonder who I or we are, or what. What planet is this
anyway, my dear? You see my confusion. I need to have
things explained. Like what we'll do tomorrow and the
next day and in our old age, discussions about little
things, miniscule matters such as the possibility of
varying the hour of breakfast, for sometimes I wish for a
sort of landmark, change, by which to commemorate
the passage of time. More coffee? In fact you might find a
bit of change would add a certain spice to your life, you
who seem determined to resist change, you who seem
to slip from one posture or gesture into another in so
mechanical a way and back again, on and on. Your
habits, my dear, I confess to find somewhat iron-bound
ever since the time when—well, whenever *that* was. I
realize of course that life on this barge is not conducive
to violent changes such as characterize the racing-car
driver's, the space man's, the political agitator's; yet you
might consider attempting to complicate our lives simply
for the experience to be gained thereby, that later in
such moments of calm like this we might have something
to talk over. What do you think?'

And what, he might wonder as he held the chattering sheet of onion-skin between his fingers, what was all
this about? I invariably neglected to say. I preferred not
to proclaim at once my innermost desires. I felt they
should be subtly drawn out of me, gently teased from
the very core of my being. Children of course; five to be
exact, an ample brood. I still did long every now and
then to see land before I died, just a scrap, any old

53

desert island, but a full-fledged continental mass if at all possible. The thought being to lead him into conversations, then from one thing to another, and to those things finally. But his reaction, equally invariable, to my carefully typed-out remarks was to award me a day off, and foolishly every time I leaped at the opportunity, swallowed the bait and resolved to wait another year before resuming negotiations. So I would go downstairs and wash up the dishes and return to deck to find Unguentine drawing in the heavy rope by which the swimming platform was towed, a thing of fat timbers strapped on to old oil drums. I remember the day. I looked over the rail; the platform was directly below the stern. We embraced. The thickness, the solidity, the sheer weight of the incarnation of our bodies together surprised me into an audible gasp. So he was there, after all. Where were my things, he indicated somberly. I produced a bag. Inside, a plastic raincoat, towel, a few home-made chocolate bars, a jar of fresh water, a flashlight; a hook, line, sinker and bait. Then I squatted on top of the railing an instant before dropping my lithe body the seven feet below to the swimming platform, which pitched under the weight of my fall. Above, Unguentine untied the orange rope and let it snake into the water with an elongated splash. I blew him a kiss, he waved, I saw children's faces pressed against the glass where there was no sun-glare, but illusions, flowers only. I heard Unguentine pull closed the stern doors. Soon we were drifting apart. The sea was still calm and the horizon slightly misted as I slipped away and beyond to the fading sounds of roosters crowing, ducks quacking, the cooing of doves, the morning noises of the barnyard with which I could feel no more connection if I so chose, a whole morning, most of a day, to lose myself and everything in the blankness of sea and sky. Soon it would all dwindle to a glaring presence on the horizon, impossible even to look at on account of the blinding reflections of the sun on the silvered panes of the dome, and I would spread out my towel on the hoary planks and lie down on my stomach, my cheek against cool wood, eyes half closed and lost in the worn depths of those planks on which the action of waves had raised a nap of soft orange fur and in whose grain there flowed currents and rivers from pool to pool, threaded with tapered sandbanks. Those planks, those logs, my vacation home with its wide cracks and through them the sound of water lapping and secret little drafts, glints of sunlight from the water licking at the barrels underneath. Hours might pass before I would finally turn my head to let the warming sun play upon my face and take a squinting look away, would wonder what could compare to the edge, the line formed by the planks against the opalescence of the morning sea, as seen naked with all body, body drinking, as body stretched farflung to contact more the warm, damp logs, my nails dug in to pick at splinters, toes caressing the sun hot upon my back. So to doze, sink deeper in; or lose it. Thus quickly a day. Once a year. My day off.

So soon sunset and out of the west, aquatic pines sighing in the wind, the flaming barge would swoop down like a proud and hissing gander to pick me up and carry me off—or the faceted eye of an insect come too close. Unguentine would be there standing on the bow with a coil of rope in hand, poised to fling it across. Often he would be balancing himself on tiptoes on the railing. I tried to discourage the habit. 'Get down off that

railing, you'll fall,' my first words shouted to him after a
day away. Fall he did, more than once. He was like that,
he would put on his tennis shoes and find some pre-
carious point to stand on with one foot, balance there
until the inevitable, humming, making little squeaks,
blowing sharp, obscene noises into the wind, until he
would fall. Once as he stood up on that rail, hopping
methodically up and down on one foot, the other
dangling over the sea, arms flexing up and down at the
elbows and rope whipping back and forth, I shouted up
at him somewhat harshly to throw down the line; it was
getting dark, there were things to be done, dinner, the
bed to be made. He attempted to give the rope a toss
while still bouncing up and down. But in that delicate
manoeuvre, the railing being perhaps slippery with an
evening dew or an invisible application of grease or oil,
he came down not on his muscular toes but on his
instep, painfully, in such a way that he lost his balance
slightly, his heel sliding from the rail, legs akimbo and
arms thrashing, coil of rope spinning way off mark and
splashing into the water, his crotch rushing inexorably
downwards towards the rail, the dull thud, the awful
blow by which any ordinary man would have thoroughly
castrated himself. I remember the way he doubled over
in pain, rolling off the rail in a compact ball. Hastily I
attempted to look the other way. Seconds later there
came the splash. What if it all ended like that, I thought,
with a stupid accident out in the middle of nowhere?
But that could never be, I knew. I fished him out, as
usual. Nothing to worry about beyond the bother of it
all, swirling hair and wet arms, sopping clothes. I
suspected him of being somewhat immortal at times.
Indestructible, surely, for he never hurt himself however

much he might have tried. Often, returning to the
barge, I sighed. For whatever happened, it would never
end. We were out of time. On and on. Forever. That
man. These seas.

VIII

After years and years of marriage, and
forever on the seas, lonely, I finally demanded a child.
I remember the day. The sky clear and hard with a hot,
dry wind foaming the crests of high waves, the barge
rolling and pitching, branches of trees snapping back
and forth. Here and there leaves and twigs, whip-
lashed free, dribbled to the ground. Unguentine had
previously removed the figurehead from the prow for a
new paint job; she was a thick-lipped and heavily
rouged creature with a fixed stare, and all bundled up
in drapery to conceal a problem of bulk; and made out
of wood. Her name, unknown. She hadn't come with
the barge. Unguentine had pulled her up out of some
shallows one day despite my caustic remarks. So there
she was. He had her inside the dome and laid out on a
tarpaulin on the lawn, had sanded her down, was repainting her. The lower lids of her big black eyes
drooped, giving her an expression of dumb terror such
as might be assumed at the prospect of imminent collision; no doubt she deserved those shallows, her long
water life. I compliment her arms, however, hanging

limply by her sides, for at least there was something
feminine about them. I shuffled around the lawn smoking while Unguentine knelt and painted. The jealousy I
was attempting to feign was mainly to clear the air.
Having spent all morning searching the garden for a
note from him. Having taken up smoking for the occasion, that he might know where I was by means of the
smoke and my frequent fits of coughing. Rhythmically
he brushed away at her red robe. 'Won't help,' I muttered. 'She's too far gone.' Such things. Every now and
then, the paint stinking, he would clear his nose with a
sharp and hissing inhalation, or draw his left wrist
across the nostrils, wiping the residue on his left hip
pocket. 'Blow your nose,' I told him more than once,
not that he could easily do so with paint all over his
hands. I was waiting for him to get it on his trousers.
Then I might really have words with him. But he refused to do either. Raised slowly but inexorably by a
huge swell, the barge crested and rumbled down the
other side, the glass of the dome chattering in its frames
and the decks shuddering as we hit bottom with a
lurch. The branches of the nearest tree, the Fir Irene,
sprang up and down. Beyond the trees, a splash, the
angry quacking of ducks. It seemed I was getting nowhere with him. I turned my back and strode away
without saying a word, down the little path laid with
driftwood through the sycamores, the lilacs, the roses,
the gladioli, past a tub of cactus, and opened the door
on to the bow and stepped outside. A brisk gale had
sprung up. The glass of the dome was all hazed over by
countless applications of salt-spray; yet it was hot out,
over ninety, with the sky now dimmed by the golden
dusts of some far desert, a land in the air. I marvelled

briefly. The most I had seen in years. With tears stream-
ing from my eyes and the wind whipping them away, I
slung my brown thighs over the rail and dropped my
feet to a ledge and groped along to the anchor as the
bow pumped up and down over the high waves and
into the valleys between, my body utterly naked to the
hot wind and cooling spray. At last I was gripping the
rusty studs which had held at the figurehead and by
which, in an instant of calm, I swung myself down to
her pedestal where I soon stood facing out to sea, my
arms stretched wide to welcome the ceaseless waters,
scraps of seaweed, fish, anything. 'Please!' I shouted,
perhaps more than once. My eyes became sealed,
closed by the howling brine wind; after each wave I
gargled and retched. Yet there was some odd security
amid all the tumult, poised as I was on the edge of a
precipice, gripping numbly, the roughness scraping
against my buttocks, and I felt I could have released my
hands or even kicked my legs so perfect was the balance
of my position, pressed between wind, waves and barge.
Or that I might be lying on a prickly earth, on my back,
staring into a fierce sun. Possibly it went on for hours.
My body vanished away into a sort of numbness for
whoever or whatever was left inside me, watching,
listening, a small creature who came to life spasmodi-
cally whenever the wind chanced to pry open my lips
and whirl down my throat, striking my vocal chords
and generating words, half-words, groans, odd scraps of
verbiage that seemed like fuzzy caterpillars or thistles
glowing many colours. But how could they have warmed
me so much? Words not even mine but only the flogging
sea's, jammed into my throat, uttered? Then vanish?
Thistles? Thistles?

I came to hours later to find myself stretched out on some blankets on the bedroom floor, with Unguentine crouching opposite me, leaning against the bulkhead with his knees drawn up to his chin. A pot of steaming tea separated us, biscuits. Outside the storm still raged. Moments like this I imagined, for comfort, that through those walls all the good and smiling people I had ever known were throwing buckets of water against the side of the barge. Unguentine now prepared to speak. I knew the gesture intimately. The manner in which he quickly wet his lips with his tongue, swallowed, opened his mouth a crack. 'What exactly is it you want, my dear?'

I rewarded him with a winning smile despite my condition. My whole face glowed. 'A child,' I said. At last I had done it, said it. Unflinchingly he poured tea and handed me a cup, also a biscuit. Brightly I awaited a response. But none came, only the sound of tea being sipped, the crunch of biscuits. Through the bulkhead came the creaks and groans of unused machinery, wardrobes and trunks shifting about. After a while he got up and left me. The storm was to last five days, at the end of which time I was recovered sufficiently to resume hanging around him, get in his way, sigh. At last a response came, or at least an acknowledgment of my request. He was searching the roses for aphids at the time. I remember his large black eyes staring at me through leaves. Shimmering leaves. He was kneeling in the dirt. He said he would see. I thought, while he spoke those words, I heard a tinkling of very fine bells or the chatter of a tambourine—but such was often the case those rare times he spoke, what with that fleshly tongue of his, that oddly musical pronunciation.

But see what? I was to puzzle at length over these

words and wonder whether by saying he would see he meant that by waiting long enough my desire might lapse, be displaced by others, such as school-teaching, baby-sitting, affection for dogs and cats; or whether he meant to deny me now in order to reward me greater some time later. Next day I ransacked his gestures for a hint of exegesis, but they were the same as always, breakfast taken standing on the stern deck at sunrise to those peculiar mutterings he made only at that hour, little squeals and groans deep in his throat, an inner sort of laughter that scarcely passed his lips, the click of tongue, the yawn, a rubbing noise he produced by kneading his bare toes on the deck, this last being a signal for those five or six gulls he had befriended and which stayed with our barge through thick and thin for the regular breakfast he now scattered into the water: some toast, a pailful of garden pests, a few slices of fresh fruit. Days passed. Idly I wandered around the barge and wondered what to do. Then for the first time in years I took to wearing clothes again, plain things, drab things, tattered, unironed. One morning, written in miniscule letters on a white speck stuck to the bathroom mirror, the message: 'Where has your body gone?' So he had noticed. I sniffed success. The night, Unguentine asleep, I flung open trunks and footlockers and dragged bundles of clothes upstairs and spread them out on bushes to air in the garden, drawing them back in before dawn like coloured mists. A day of secret ironing and mending. Next morning, I arrived late and haughty to the breakfast table, wrapped in the dazzling lavenders of a full-length evening gown as if I had spent the whole night dancing with dark and hairy men. Unguentine tried to pretend nothing was the matter. But I saw his whiskers billow in and out with the heavy breathing of irritation, I saw him twice spill his coffee. On I went. Seemingly from nowhere, I would make my apparition in the garden and glide slowly between trees, my oiled body lathered in veils. Decked out in flowers and a too-short pinafore, I swung back and forth in our garden swing, lisping infantile lullabies. In buckskin loincloth and feathered bra I climbed trees and criticized his lawn-mowing in shrewish pidgin English, pelted him with ripe fruit. Or he would be down in the hold sealing a leak in the hull when, quietly, from out of the darkness, a soft and grease-smeared form clad in overalls would roll past him to vanish into another darkness. Once I dabbed myself with ketchup and old scraps of material and draped myself over the winch, as if with leg caught in the gears. One whole afternoon I spent making up my eyelids to resemble my eyes, in such a way that when closed they appeared to be wide open; I confronted him with this phenomenon at dinner, the seemingly blink-less stare; he bolted his dinner and ran.

A week I performed in this manner, then disappeared into the lushest corner of the garden with a set of long mirrors for a painstaking application of iridescent body paint, with an effect of mother-of-pearl all over my body except for breasts and buttocks which I finished off in a brilliant matt orange. Thus adorned I fasted in seclusion a day and a night, and came to know inwardly that my time was near. As the sun rose the next day through the dome I planted myself in the center of the lawn and began the rhythmic beating of gongs; there was incense, perfume, and I even had a pot of coffee warming on a charcoal brazier behind a bush and some coffee-cake wrapped in tinfoil. An hour passed. The gongs grew heavy. Then the rustle of leaves somewhere in the depths of the garden. I nearly fainted. The slow and scarcely audible pad of bare feet. At last. He had understood. There he was, striding naked from the trees, his organ full and erect and painted purple, his beard dyed green, dark body powdered with what might have been flour, a thunderhead moving near among the long and rich shadows of sunrise. He stood before me. He nudged me once with his organ and said, 'Are you fertile?' 'I am,' I replied. With a sweeping gesture meant perhaps to encompass the whole barge, gardens, all, he then asked, 'Do you know what it will mean?' 'I certainly do not,' I snapped, impatient to get on with it, not discuss it. And so we fell to making love. I had tied our motion picture camera to a branch especially for the occasion; it now whirred gently. Our dogs, sensing an event taking place, came and sat respectfully at a distance at the edge of the lawn, bright eyes with flicking, hairy lids and limp, swinging tongues, panting. Soon they were joined by the cat and the goat, also some of the chickens, one of the ducks. I gasped; he grunted. There was no orgasm, there was only orgasm from beginning to end. I remember shrieking in the middle of some night traversed noisily at high speed: 'I am conceiving!' From Unguentine, a low and rhythmic groan, a syllable mouthed over the course of an hour, a morning, with the rising sun burning into our bodies on the lawn; I see him suddenly in spasms, then rolling away in the grass, perhaps hissing, 'I have generated . . .' We lay immobile, separated, until nearly noon, until the neglected barge drew us to our feet. We embraced once briefly, and while he bent about his business in the garden, I withdrew below to tend to my pregnancy.

As for our child to be, I already knew he would be a girl: manchild while within my belly, but a girl once born. I made up lists of names and posted them around the barge for Unguentine's approval. Beatrude? Marygret? Gertrice? Barbarence? Nancice? Jilly? I wove a set of little blankets on a loom. Speedily I knitted what few clothes she would need between birth and age six. Long hours I lay in the sun on my back, that my belly might rise like yeasted dough. Unguentine spent days below deck partitioning off a section of the hold for the baby's room, boring a hole in the hull that she might have her own porthole and for which I sewed up a set of curtains. Peaceful days, still and calm days of quiet work, with all time stopped and only gentle, distant intimations of nibblings, flight, panic, the rush of emergencies. Arm in arm we would stroll about the garden by day, brush through banks of flowers, our hair caressed by the needles of overhanging boughs, our bare feet padding upon wood, upon stone, upon grass, the metal of the deck; now and then we would stand close to the windows and peer out to sea, whitecaps and troughs of cobalt. I remember that midnight on the bow, anchors dropped, a moon casting a strange simulacrum of day-light over the water through some haze in the sky, a tone of light almost identical to that of a foggy day; and we stood at the railing which glistened under the slight-est application of dew, the sea being waveless and graced only by lazy swells that passed us like the undu-lations of a great caterpillar's back; and it was then, spontaneously, that we both broke into song, into a lilting sort of aria, but unsyllabled and smooth and which trailed off into a low hum, charging the night sea until the horizon bubbled with sheet-lightning and the waters glowed with the pulsations of electronic plankton, and we fell silent. Unguentine trembled; I nestled closer to his warm body. He was about to speak, I sensed, knowing the signs. He did finally, to announce quietly that he would deliver the baby. I confided that I had never dreamed of anyone else, being so far from all land now.

However, a month passed when there took place an event such that I realized I was not pregnant after all— and I not pregnant with a husband who measured my girth with a tape-measure each night before bed was in a perilous position, or so I felt. I had no way of knowing. Unguentine, it seemed, was frankly worshipping my womb. One morning I arose somewhat earlier than usual and spotted him kneeling on the stern deck. I approached softly, on bare feet. But my toe brushed against an empty paint can which let out a raucous clang. His back doubled, his arms swooping in. I saw candles. I saw a shiny tin form, bulbous and horned. An embroidered cloth. But he scurried away, all his objects of devotion bundled pell-mell into the cloth from which billowed the black smoke of candles still lit, and he vanished round a corner, coughing. At other times he seemed to be in the grip of a peculiar depression and took to napping lengthily in an ugly tent-like shelter made out of old carboard boxes, as if to shut out the splendours of the dome. The Plum Patricia, a heavily bearing tree from which I made my best jam, suddenly vanished one day; no explanation, no remains even, other than a shattered stump in the ground that spoke of cyclones, whirlwinds. I didn't know what to do, what to say. As if to spare me the necessity of confronting him with my sad news he would go into seclusion somewhere on the barge for days on end, presumably in one of his several hiding-places I had discovered beneath the lawn, entered through a trap-door in the turf, invisible until that day he took up smoking down there and wispy plumes revealed its place and shape; the solar distillation tank, in disuse since the advent of our floating lake, which he entered by means of a hatch on its underside, apparently unaware that the sounds of his breathing were perfectly transmitted by the empty pipes and loudly broadcast all over the galley through the cold water tap, the familiar humming, squeaks, all his other odd noises. Or, his most prized place and favourite haunt, a nest way up in the crown of the Chestnut Anna, and many times I have chanced to watch him, thinking himself unseen, climb the trunk in the early morning and crawl out on one of the middle branches, then reach up and part a cluster of leaves and hoist himself up to a small platform. Once settled on it, he would draw the branches around him with rein-like ropes in such a way that he was completely concealed from the ground or from the dome above, a beautiful thing to see, this drawing in of the leaves around him like a flower closing for the night. Before he vanished each day he would wind up a dozen old alarm clocks hidden away in the hold, which actuated an elaborate network of piano wires and little mallets all over the barge, and which would generate a day's worth of uncanny noises in unlikely places, the sound of a hedge being clipped, the brief clatter of tools being picked up or laid down, the *tap-tap* of something being driven in, worked at, broken up, distinct and life-like sounds no doubt meant to comfort me during those long hours of his absence, and that I might not try to find his hiding-places. Kind man.

I never disillusioned him. I knew about it even as he secretly installed the wires, and quietly I admired the complicated mechanisms, pendulums, gyroscopes, that enabled the system to work even in rough weather and kept it from being set off accidentally with him sitting but inches away from me.

Unable to find him for days on end and unable to speak the words to him when he finally emerged from seclusion, I took to the wearing of clothes again and would not be touched; I strapped a specially sewn pillow around my middle, and above all I ate and ate, became shy. The second month I began to put on weight all over, a silky plumpness, tight and firm except for my thighs with their dimpled slackness, but only I saw that. Unguentine soon noticed, soon glowed; I was happy for him, at least. He prohibited me from all manual work and labour. He spied on me through keyholes and cracks in order to discover my cravings. A hankering glance cast at a food cupboard would bring him bursting through the hatchway five minutes later, staggering under a heaped platter of whatever he thought I might then desire. Bananas? Peanuts? Avocadoes? Milk shakes? Chocolate cakes? And he would sit there, eyes wide with adoration and fascination, until I finished the last crumb and drop. The raw materials of our child, I thought I heard him say once. Stoke the furnaces! Chew, woman, chew! The more weight I gained and the more I grew, the happier Unguentine seemed to become and the more food he prepared for me, cheeses, yoghurts, all the fruits and nuts and vegetables our barge-garden was then bearing, rare delicacies made from herbs and honeys, special preparations of kelp and algae. But this could not go on. In three months I gained a hundred

69

pounds. One hot day as I reclined perspiring under a fir tree near the lawn, as I lay there obese and barren, a beached walrus, panting, fanning myself, I wondered through my tears how I was possibly ever going to get out of this, how I could ever discharge myself of his expectations. Even now as I lay there Unguentine was rigging up nearby a low-lying contraption of wood and canvas—a great fan, it turned out, which beat towards me with wings like those of a butterfly at rest; and to its slow pulsations and the waves of air washing over my tears and beads of sweat I composed elaborate speeches I would never have the courage to utter to my poor husband, whose life was now only an impatient wait for all my populations. 'My dear,' I would say to him and did even type it all out, 'concerning my pregnancy I would like to make an observation or two, a remark. I have the feeling it might not be *taking*, for example that the sperm might not have been sufficiently strong to break through the shell of the egg, preferring rather to simply lie beside it. Resulting in a pregnancy rather too spiritual for the coarser mechanisms of my body which searched and longed for the less-nuanced form, the direct *yes*, the blunt *no*, without *maybe*, without *perhaps*, without *in part*. Therefore I conclude that though egg and sperm came together they did not in fact ever meld into one—though in being somewhat less than two, my ignorant body so interpreted their quasi-union and thus initiated this whole sequence of events which I now believe is leading us absolutely nowhere. owhere. where. here. ere. re. e.'

But how could I ever say such a thing to a man who was spending whole days in elaborate preparations for the day of birth? Who was installing a dozen signalling

70

cannon on the decks of the barge, to be fired off upon
the birthday dawn, perhaps opposite some great port
where friends still lived but whom now in my shame I
never wanted to see again? Who was building an amazing series of twelve cradles, the smallest being for the
first month, the largest for the twelfth, and which all
fitted together in such a way that, when stored, the
whole lot took up no more room than the twelfth alone,
and which, beyond the twelfth month, could be effort-
lessly refitted to form little houses, wagons, boats, trains,
and which finally, after age twelve, could be stacked
against the wall as a pyramid-shaped bookshelf? As a
planter? How could I say? How? I could not. One night
when I was still ambulatory, the sixth or seventh month,
I complained of insomnia and sent Unguentine below
deck to bed so that I might wander the gardens alone in
my misery and flabby unworthiness, and it was then
that I resolved to escape at last and leave this barge and
the gardens and Unguentine and launch myself into the
blackness of the night, forever. I knew now I no longer
deserved this life with him I had so often cursed for
that aura of bland eventlessness which had seemed to
surround him and all his works, those old accusations
that he never did anything, that nothing ever happened
to him, that it just went on and on. Here was an event
now, an awful event: my failure. What was I amongst his
subtle tools of light and air, water, growth, decay? A
parasite, a parasite bloated near to madness with over-
eating. So I loaded up our little skiff with jugs of water
and cartons of dried fruit, a few biscuits, a change of
clothes that might come to fit me again after several
weeks of wasting away at sea, an umbrella, a pair of
high-heeled shoes, and, as future memento of all that

would have been, a pot of geraniums. As I stood there on deck, the night pitch-black, flashlight trained on the skiff's little cargo complete now but for myself and ready to be lowered into the water, I remembered all the times I had jumped ship decades before and gone and hid far away from that man, in cities, in hard, unyielding landscapes. I wondered often how he always found me, why he always came and got me. Those weeks of utter silence back on the barge. Days I would lie in bed, refusing even food. Then forget. Forget it all. When now I found myself unable to move. Except, weeping, to cast the contents of the skiff into the sea, and lie down on the deck to be swept over by the cooling breezes of night.

Still it went on and on. I could not speak the words. The ninth month I lay in a special three-ply heavy-duty hammock Unguentine had slung between two trees, the Plane Trees Martha and Judith, I lay there swinging back and forth, I lay with a horrible 250-pound excrescence coagulated upon my frail bones, unable to walk, unable even to see my feet, occasionally flapping my fleshly arms for exercise or to speed the swinging of the hammock to and fro. Above me, amid translucent trees, birds twittered. Birds! That an ounce of flesh and bones and feathers could not only fly but could sing as well— so very much! An ounce! And I, an eighth of a ton avoirdupois. I wept. That afternoon, in my ninth month, I remembered in a sort of delirium my every mouthful of food, I remembered its harvesting, its preparation, its cooking, I traced the genealogy of tiny seeds back into a past without memory, and all I wanted to do was vomit it back to earth, for I had taken and eaten what was not mine, upon false pretences. Night fell. Someone must have closed the dome windows. I had not seen Unguen-

72

tine all day. The sea being rough that night, the hammock swung back and forth to the sharp creaking of ropes and the groan of branches under strain, my bottom dragging on the lawn and wearing an ugly sore in the grass. I resolved then, no matter the cost or the consequences, to tell Unguentine the truth first thing in the morning and begin fasting immediately thereafter.

At 3 a.m. however I was roused from sleep by a sharp clicking noise followed by a floodbath of light. Grunting, I raised my head and squinted around at the gardens completely illuminated from lamps concealed in the earth, and with that peculiar effect of vegetal nudity that comes from brightness playing on the underside of leaves. Then the familiar metal clank and grinding noises, ratchets and chains, and there, to the other side of the lawn, the rising hook-like form of the freight elevator, and Unguentine's head. He had been using the freight elevator to bring me up food prepared in the galley, also to take me down below for my daily bath; now I closed my eyes, clenched my teeth and fortified my resolve. Not a bite. Not one. I could hear his footsteps. Perhaps he knew. Perhaps he was coming to murder me. I deserved it. I had brought it all upon myself. I could feel his hand steadying the swinging hammock. 'Open your eyes,' he said softly. I did. I gasped. For there, before me, in his outstretched arms, was a perfectly formed nine-month-old baby, grandly sexed as male, and staring at me thoughtfully. Such eyes. I fainted.

I came to as the dome of night above me, above the plane trees, pulsated and glinted with the outrageous colours of Unguentine's home-made fireworks whose detonations set the five hundred panes into a frenzy of rattling. The sea, calm and moonless, responded with ripples of reflection, drank flames. At dawn the twenty cannon blasted away until exhausted. And through all this the child slept, tiny creature in a cradle bedecked with gaping orchids. From the trees Unguentine finally emerged again. He was covered head to toe with soot, his overalls in a shambles. It was a magnificent moment. On the grass we were to lie all together then, the three of us, for hours while I learned from Unguentine the number of nappies per day, the preparation of the child's cereal and vegetables, milk, his sleeping hours, his periods of optimum petulance, his attitudes towards sun, baths, drafts, ice, fire. But no name. Unguentine refused. To name, he said, would be to clasp the near and present end of the chain called history and thus to forge another link, and how sad! I agreed. He remained nameless. Child, baby, son. Quite enough terms to cover his condition. He spoke early and ignored both our admonitions, Unguentine's that he should seek silence and speak not at all, mine that he should speak only the purest of truths at whatever length he wished to do so up to twenty-four hours a day; instead he turned out to be an average talker, a casual but charming liar by virtue of averagely not knowing what to say during that always crucial moment, of talking constantly in hindsight and in foresight and thereby eating up more and more of the endless time now, though with what a sweet voice, my God! He matured a genius at five, became an excellent swimmer, grew modest and swam away one day, no doubt having had his fill of us, the barge, these seas.

IX

The barge, magnificent barge, a jewel
cresting upon the high seas those thirty to forty years
when the weather was still a true marvel, when one
could see stars at noon, when the rare clouds were so
fine and gauze-like and so much more transparent to
moons, when rains were frank and without whining
drizzle and cleared without lingering—such was the
bright and empty space we sailed across seemingly to no
end, and where my simple chores could have gone on
for days and days without me minding—there could
never be too many decks to sweep and wash, too many
sails to mend, too many windows to clean amid that
everlasting radiance. I remember the morning, if it is the
one, that I brought the dishpan up from the galley in
order to wash the dishes out in the rising sun and cool
breeze of the stern deck, the galley being hot and steamy
and infested with one of our infrequent plagues of
crickets and cockroaches. Unguentine knew about them,
would be down there this very moment unleashing the
domestic snakes. By noon the galley would be all cleaned
out and the reptiles, fat and lethargic, put back in their

cages out of my sight. Are you sure? I always asked. Did you count them? You checked the dark corners to make sure they did no breeding down there? He would nod reassuringly. Meanwhile I went on with the dishes, clearing them off the table and tossing the scraps overboard into the water of our fresh-water lake fluorescent green with strands of algae, the water-cress and water-lilies where perched and floated heavy, complacent bullfrogs with fast tongues, strange body of water which swelled and shrank in size according to some principle I never grasped, changes in temperature perhaps. But the air, which had seemed clear and fresh before I went below deck for the dishpan, now was gathering up a humid haze, tarnishing the sea beyond our lake with a scum-like effect such as I could not remember having seen in years; or in the drowsiness of early morning I had simply not noticed: perhaps it had even been with us for days. I was out of time. I hadn't slept well the night before, had mistakenly attempted a midnight stroll through the gardens in the dark only to walk right into a field of ripe peaches and apricots fallen on the ground, the awful squishing noises beneath my bare feet, the slime and stickiness, and from which I finally ran slipping and screaming to the lawn where I was able to light a candle and hose myself off. Why I refused to eat any fruit that morning. Our abundance at times was gagging. I was grown too plump anyway, though it was all still firm this body of mine, spangled with the reflections of wavelets in the dishpan, naked in the sun, every bone and muscle ceaselessly active and fresh, my skin tanned to a glowing sienna with only a vein surfacing here and there near a breast, a wrist, an instep, to indicate the warm flood which sometimes seemed to flow out and beyond, to feed the rainbow colours of it all, dishpan and stern deck, our lake, the sea, back to the sun.

Unguentine was in his prime those days, he was more present, more carnal, his body exuding the manly aromas of ripe glands so strongly I could nose out his shifts in mood, the nature of his work, for hours at a time even though he might be at the far end of the barge. He never spoke, no longer wrote me notes. I didn't need them. I would read his face and body, and he mine, to know what thoughts were to traverse the narrow band of air which separated our flesh. From a hand lying loosely on the table, palm nearly exposed, perhaps trembling slightly with the pulse within, I heard repose and the silence of no thought. From the half-tightened fist seeming to indicate rest but being only an interlude, I heard the chatter of little plans before he would spring to his feet and slip into the garden—to do God knows what, for our trees and flowers and vegetables grew by themselves in a weedless, springy humus which needed no tending beyond the regular harvests that only permitted them to grow more, did not empty the garden, did not ravish it. We had too much, in fact. Often while pulling up a head of lettuce and a few carrots and onions for the simple salad-dinner we would have that night, I wearied at the thought of what we might possibly do with those rows upon rows of vegetables which would not stop growing and which we mainly fed to the chickens and goats, only to be swamped with eggs and milk and cupboards crammed with cheeses—dumped finally overboard to feed the fish. The balance of nature we carried about with us wherever we sailed was so perfect, so precise that were Unguentine and I to leave it all for ten years, say on some excursion to land at last, upon our return we would find nothing changed, perhaps only the trees grown a little higher, hens a different colour, the cold and glassy stare of another goat or two. Even, days like this, sky becoming whiter and the air more humid, I felt pressed down by the thought we might be intruders on this barge, for one could not sink a hoe into our earth without slicing up at least half a dozen earthworms and grubs, and then, that done, be surrounded by a gathering of robins anxious to feast. Flies would hatch in the compost heap and live long enough to lay more eggs before being pounced on by spiders, snatched up by swallows; and then the visitations of hawks and shrikes that thinned the swallows and sparrows and lizards and frogs while we watched, perhaps only watched. I knew the necessity, our carrots and onions, peaches and cream; yet sometimes I wished it would simply all cease.

I had just finished washing the dishes when I heard an awful clatter from the bow. I thought for a moment we had run aground or collided with some metallic debris—until I recognized it as the long-unfamiliar sound of the anchor being lowered. A few minutes later the clatter resumed, shaking the barge stem to stern, followed by the lowering of the second anchor: we had two. A flush of annoyance flooded over me. Here? In this scummy sea with its haze-filled sky? No doubt Unguentine had his reasons, repairs to be made on the hull, the rudder adjusted. Still, he might have waited until we had reached a more pleasant climate. The barge had been in continual motion so long that I now felt quite dizzy and had to go below deck to lie down in our bedroom where the only living, crawling thing was myself, in the silent darkness. I could become oppressed by the incessant noises of things growing and dropping up there, the busy chatter of birds and gnawing of insects; it was as if all the creatures had flown inside my head to bat about there, to become brain cells spluttering trivial messages at each other, back and forth, to no end. I slept, however. When I emerged several hours later, refreshed by a dreamless time below, an old excitement was returning to me as I stepped into the gardens again—and saw Unguentine wrestling with the trunk of the Plane Tree Judith. I heard a crack, saw a bluish glint of metal. Unguentine sprang away from the tree-trunk. He must have seen me then; he waved his arms violently, and I turned and ran, pursued by a hissing roar that gave way to a thunderous crash. From all over the barge came the rising crescendo of livestock in panic; birds, flushed from their haunts and seeking to rise to the safety of open sky, fluttered and banged against the glass of the dome. I had taken shelter behind the Fir Irene, now peeped out. The Plane Tree Judith lay prone all over the lawn, her crown staring me in the face. Beyond, through leaves drooping at unaccustomed angles, Unguentine stood leaning against an axe, body glistening with sweat.

I approached him. At his feet, a huge saw, wedges. A little pruning, my dear? Thinning things out a bit? Perhaps such things I asked him, whether I spoke them or not as I gazed down at my favourite tree, into whose foliage I had often peered from atop the dome, into the soft and changing greens, when I was weary of looking at the harsh glitter of the sea. He must have known that. He must have heard the little cries within my heart even as he stepped away from me, dragging his tools behind him, granting me one long glance before he

79

raised the axe to limb the fallen tree, eyes clouded and narrowed with a shadowy determination I had never seen in him, or with a sadness I thought we had forever chased from our lives. I felt a sudden lassitude, exhaustion. I knew somehow then that the Plane Tree Judith would not be the last. Something had happened. I could not understand those garbled noises that came from within his heaving body—if there was anything to be heard beyond the frantic stretch and pull of muscles, the squeak of joints, a heart pounding furiously. That day and the next and beyond, despite the sweltering temperatures of the tropical sea where we lay anchored, he cut down, limbed and sawed up the other plane tree, the Fir Irene, the Beech Cynthia, the stately Elm Myra, all the fruit trees but two; and, with the wrenching crack of each falling trunk, another flower bed, another shrub, another vine was smashed and battered to the ground; a duck was killed in one of the falls, the chickens gave up laying. Gritting my teeth to hold in a somehow angerless hysteria, I helped rake up leave and toss branches overboard until I could no longer bear it and went below deck wondering how I would ever be able to set foot in the gardens again. It was impossible to believe: to ruin so utterly the work of thirty to forty years in ten days? It was beyond reason, beyond madness. Was this Unguentine, my Unguentine of the flowing white hair and yellow beard who had tended the gardens into all their magnificence? How could I watch the axe raised above his head and warmly feel his whole body tensed and poised for a perfectly delivered slice, the blur of a sudden movement, the blow, yellow chip spinning away—how could I still follow his every gesture with such fascination, then to collapse with trembling at

80

the thought of what he was actually carrying out? He was cutting wood, I tried to tell myself, only cutting wood, for we might be sailing soon to colder seas and would need heat, fat logs for the fireplace, Irene, kindling, Cynthia. Or, the trees were being cut down, but not by Unguentine: it was some other, someone else, another man whom I had never personally met, never wished to.

He left me alone in my seclusion. He prepared my meals in the galley and set them on a tray in front of the bedroom door, adding every other night a pair of clean sheets, for even the normally cool depths of the barge were infected with the oppressive heat; I could open the porthole only at midnight to catch a brief, cool breeze that sprang up about then. Days I numbly watched the sickly sea through glass and longed for the moment when the barge would sink with a rush of waves and broken glass and settle to a quiet place below, waveless, dark, cold, as surely it would have to some day: the sooner the better. I stripped the bedroom of all its furnishings except the bed, a pitcher of water, a basin, and stuffed everything through the porthole in the middle of the night, rugs, tapestries, hangings I had once spent months weaving. For the first time in years I wanted Unguentine to come to me, explain, soothe me with torrents of words—not that any of it could undo what had been done, but only for the comfort of another voice until the intoxication of words might lead us on to do what little remained to be done, if anything, and face the earth and leaves and branches as they were, without noise, purely, quietly. I wove happy fantasies of how he would replant all the trees with fresh saplings, and we would watch them grow high again, twice as fast as before; again to be cut, again to grow. I ventured into

81

dreams of setting foot on an empty beach with white sands, but withdrew after a brief visit filled with vertigo and a handful of small seashells, useless souvenirs, for now, with so many years at sea, I knew I could live no other way than what had been if I were to live at all, with the wind through the trees and the thirst of the prow for endless waves.

When, two weeks later, my solitude having placed me in a state of resignation in which I thought I could bear anything, Unguentine strode through the bedroom door with bright eyes and a smile that seemed to indicate nothing had ever happened—I burst into tears and fiercely wished nothing ever had. We embraced. I apologized for having stripped the bedroom, chattered on about this and that, old conversations, ancient words that uncontrollably came across the years and back to me. He didn't seem to mind. Soon I was following him upstairs towards the gardens. I hadn't wanted to go, not so quickly. I wondered whether it was really my Unguentine I was behind, or some arrogant, hirsute creature whose biped tramping set the whole staircase to clattering. I dreaded the first look. Desert? Dustbowl? Bomb crater? Unaccustomed to the flood of bright light beneath the dome, I was to wander around uncomprehending a half hour until his gestures and demonstrations made clear what he had done. A few trees he had spared; why I didn't know, no more than I knew why he had cut the others down, why he had begun replacing them with ones of his own creation, dry and brittle mimics which yet caught the contour of trunk and branch framework, the traceries of twig, needle, bud—why this fake forestry? I was stunned. Upon armatures of steel rod he had woven coils of rope fifty and sixty feet into the air, padded them with kapok and foam rubber, glued and stitched them up with simulated barks of dried and shredded kelp, bound and applied in the manner of papier-mâché. The leaves, plastic, of a two-ply lamination enclosing a liquid solution that gave them a flickering motion in breezes and winds and an uncanny translucence, almost too leaf-like. The tools and materials of his handiwork littered the remains of the living garden; I saw petunias gasping for air from beneath piles of iron rod, grapes bleeding under heaps of half-rotted rope; upended tree stumps, sacks of cement, gaping holes in the lawn where were to be sunk the steel roots of the next crop of artificial trees. I leaned on him repeatedly, his warm flesh, and sobbed; to be with him again, but also at these, his monstrosities.

Yet there was nothing to do but go on, wherever it all might lead. After a day of rest in the sticky sun, I began to help him. Something to do. He showed me how to paint the leaves. Gave me a little box of paints. Brushes. A pot of glue. A hamper of unpainted leaves the colour of skimmed milk, and slowly they began to pass through my fingers for their spatterings of green, then to be fastened to twigs of molybdenum wire and into drooping sprays along the lines indicated by his rough sketches, only a few dozen leaves a day at first, then with practice over two hundred, from one basket to another through my increasingly deft fingers, leaving small callouses and arid memories. Thence into branches and boughs to be stacked around a naked trunk, to be hoisted up and bolted on with the insidious clicking of a ratchet wrench, until a calm morning just before sunrise when the light was soft and easy to work under, a high tree ready to be inaugurated, Unguentine would climb the ladder and shift the leaves of a bough here and there to my hand signals down below, tilting them, bending them, giving a branch a vigorous shake to see how it would hang after a wind. Then he would come down to hook up the paint sprayer, re-ascend with a long red rubber tube dangling behind him and vanish into the depths of the leaves to straddle a branch while I would wait below on the lawn holding the large mirror by which he could see how his spraying appeared at a distance. The whole tree would tremble and creak as he positioned himself; then, up there somewhere, leaves would part and I might glimpse his face, eyes rolling as he struggled to unkink the hose, unclog the spray gun. A hand would droop out, point left. I'd hold up the mirror in the direction indicated. His arm reaching way out through the foliage with the nozzle pointed at a cluster of leaves whose greens were perhaps still too poisonous, he would pull the trigger, *psst-psst*, and suddenly the spot would harmonize. On to the next he would go, branches springing up and down, until gradually the whole tree would be muted with a subtle haze, like dew, like dust, and until the sun would swell up over the horizon and the dome creak to the influx of light and heat, elements for which the new trees had no use. When finished, he would climb down and walk around the trunk once or twice, his head thrown back, frowning, squinting up at it. I might go, Eh-ah, feign enthusiasm. I hated the stench of fresh paint. Some days this would be the most I saw of him. We rarely spoke. The communications I received from him were orders mainly. Do this, do that. Shear the goat, weave a rug. Air the hold. Dig up the onions, potatoes. There was no rest.

Unguentine was either busy cutting down the last of the living trees of any size, with the shambles of tangled branches, broken windows, with wandering furrows all over the yard where heavy logs had been dragged to the bow to be dropped overboard, or was wiring up their mechanical replacements, each one more ambitious, more intricate than the last. In the place of the Chestnut Anna, the most splendid of his trees when alive, there came to stand a silent and gracefully swaying thing with specially articulated boughs that needed a daily lubrication in windy weather or high seas. The leaves of the Beech Cynthia turned bright yellow after a month as the top coat of green paint flaked off in invisible specks, revealing the autumnal undercoat; and I thought we would be seeing her like that forever, paralyzed in splendour, until one morning, a morning that promised to be quiet and eventless, for there were no more large trees to be cut and the garden was now overcrowded with mechanical trees and no space left, thank God: I knew I would suffocate with any more lifelessness about. We were crossing the lawn together, just having had breakfast, in a silence that was not morose but over which seemed to hang the understanding that if only time might pass a little faster, then all might be well; and it was then that Unguentine stepped away from my side and reached over to the artificial Beech Cynthia, pulled something, a lever perhaps, and all of a sudden from up high the air resounded with a flurry of clicking noises followed by a rushing shower. I flung my arms over my head. I screamed perhaps—while every one of her thousands of leaves dropped to the ground at once with the sound of wet noodles. Then it was all over. Perhaps he said something about their needing changing, repainting. But I wasn't listening, or was listening only to the sad popping noises the laminated leaves made as crushed beneath my aimless feet, their yellow solution spurting out to stain the lawn. So this was how it would be. Year after year. Grinding them all up. Bleaching the plastic powder. Mixing up a new solution. Rolling them out like dough, cutting the leaf forms anew. The lamination. Injecting the liquid solution. Painting one side, then the other. So on, so forth, through artificial springs and painted autumns, tree by tree, the mindless work waxing and varnishing our bodies into ages too old to bear, the hideous leaves burying us and everything we had ever known under matted, impermeable mounds.

It couldn't end like this: I wouldn't have it, would kill myself first. The olden days of our youth had promised more and I still remembered the times from which we had sprung, before everything changed, when people looked so much better, the young looked younger, the old looked older as if having lived in the heat of the fields, knowing dust. Perhaps none of it had ever been living, but I would remember it so, had to. Little enough of it, true. Scraps. Flashes. I remembered something about having first fallen in love with Unguentine by image, say the fleeting reflection of a newspaper photograph in a pond, in some park, as perhaps carried by a passer-by who must have folded the paper away into his coat pocket just as I might have been hastening to catch up and have a closer look. I would have been young and pubescent then, without the courage to tug at the man's sleeve. But the image left some mark, would not vanish, stayed with me through those long years until one summer on a crowded beach I first heard Unguentine's voice while I lay buried in hot sand with my eyes shielded by sunglasses, neither awake nor asleep. The cry, that hoarse cry torn from the fast-running figure of a man who, perceiving me only the last instant before his bare feet would have trampled me, leaped into the air, over me, and ran on. It was him, I think, a thrashing shape receding so fast towards a horizon blinding with luminous sand, surf, foam; and who, I knew, would some day return. He must have. Things must have happened one after the other, to this, the barge, the mechanical forest, to the moment not long after that he disappeared once and for all in some confidential manner I never learned of; but at the right time, I suppose, somewhat late even, for he must have been just as emptied by it all as I was. He heard me, no doubt. Go. Leave now, before it is too late.

I reproached him only for leaving me after forty years together without word, without note, without explanation, scene, quarrel, bloody drama. How dare he? He knew my tastes. He knew that I should have preferred some rich terminal event such as a foot placed with seeming carelessness on a weakened pane of glass high up on the dome, the tinkle, the shout, the long fall through plastic leaves to the lawn, at my feet, where I might be weeding: the crumpled form, my dead husband fallen from the sky. Or how much I would have mulled over and enjoyed and finally treasured up in memory a scene on the stern deck as he might have lowered himself into the skiff or diving bell or simply jumped into the water with stones tied to his ankles, my shrill abuse about the marriage vows and what was to become of me now, an emptied woman upon a rudderless, leaking barge with worn-out lawns and exhausted livestock? What was I to do? Where go? Did it not use to

be that a gentleman of a man would have at least repaired the machinery before leaving so I could possibly
get somewhere? Your duty, Unguentine? He failed me. If
in fact I would have had the strength to rise to such an
occasion; as likely not. And just as likely there might
have been some little parting scene so quiet and muted I
was the one who failed to note its import at the time, as
at breakfast that day when he stood up from the table
and brushed a tea-leaf from his lip while through the
open dome doors there came the sound of the twin
sycamores' leaves slapping and grinding together like
jeering applause, and when he bent down and kissed
me once on the forehead before walking away down the
deck, jauntily, in the manner of one who has ten miles
to cover on foot before noon. Thus he vanished from
sight around the dome. I sat in my chair, finished my tea
secure in the knowledge that there was no place to go.
This was it. For months I remained convinced he would
return somehow, come back, hear me tell of what had
happened in his absence. He never did.

A year passed. Across that heavy, scummy sea the
barge drifted, surrounded by an ossuary of logs that
would not sink, as I tended the vegetables that still grew,
the goats, the seven ducks, four hens. A few more
shrubs went brown in the leaves, died. Daily I swept the
barge stem to stern, scraped off a greenish growth that
blossomed on the outside of the hull and which I
thought might be responsible for the slight list to the
left the barge was taking; these, my humble, helpless
navigations. I wired the leaves back on to the Beech
Cynthia in such a way they would never fall off. I
repainted the bedroom. Every now and then I would
crawl over the sacks of potatoes stored in the cargo hold

and wind up the alarm clocks so as to have at least the consolation of his typical noises with me, puncuate my vigil, help me sleep. The night of the first anniversary of his disappearance, or of the date I first missed him and when I hauled a forty-year-old calendar out of hiding and made a mark at random on some day and month, I went out to the stern deck and turned on the neon lights he had once wired up all over the outside of the dome, and I stood there flashing them on and off, night sea shimmering under their traceries all the colours of the rainbow. But from the darkness, from reflections like pulsating electric lotuses, there came no response. Only the ducks, awakened by the false dawn, chortled and quacked. Could it then be? Like this?

X

Years passed. Eons. Eras without temples.
Through rusting twigs, through the struts of the dome
gnawed annually higher by daring termites, the sun rose,
fell, rose; things flaked, things peeled, things vanished
into earth and mud and brackish water, into the formless
cocoon to be mixed and moulded into whatever had the
energy to sprout through and have another go. I had
seen it all before. It was the same awake, the same
asleep. I knew by heart that if in daytime the wind blew
strong and flattened the blades of grass out on the
marsh, then at night it would drop and the air be silent,
or that a cooling breeze would always follow a hot day,
dispel the haze. Yet I did what I could. A year I spent
catching up with all the correspondence neglected over
the decades, that my old friends might have some
notion of what had finally become of me and how my
life had turned out, how I came to live in seclusion
among old mirrors and deep carpets, endless chambers,
atop some highest building in a great and angry city into
whose concert halls I was limousined once a month, to
hear a gloomy symphony; how I lived in exile, in oases,

behind ramparts of palms and aqueducts and spraying
fountains, walls inlaid with intricate tiles, in the middle
of a blazing desert inhabited only by morose brigands
whose camels had the gout, how I fed them dates,
taught their children French; or my life in northern
mountains, the great stone house set amid trackless miles
of evergreens half buried in the snow nine months of
the year, the walls upstairs and down lined with books,
my reading, my lives, my lies I told them all. For I could
not speak of the sea. The sea was there, was all, beyond
the mud and ooze of the floating marsh, too close to be
chattered about. When I finally sealed up those hundred and fifty letters pasted with the bankrupt republic's
worthless postage stamps which depicted the S.S. *The
Mrs Unguentine* cutting through the waves in all her
ancient splendour, a tiny smear of dots and hatchmarks
to the right forming two seated figures, perhaps Unguentine and I at the breakfast table granting a cheerful
salute with waving arms, again and again, a hundred
and fifty times, those arms, licked, pasted, cancelled
away under the postmark once bestowed upon me,
honorary postmistress of the high seas, and which read
simply BARGE. I tied them all up into bundles and
sealed them inside a sheet of plastic, then fitted them
into a wooden box roped with life preservers. There
were still pools of water around the barge, narrow
estuaries which flowed out to sea and sometimes ran
sweet, sometimes salty; I dropped the box into one of
these and watched it float away. It didn't get far. Fifty
yards at the most, where it ran aground on a mudbank
and stayed forever after.

The barge called, however. My health was perfect, my
body the repository of a long life of vigorous exercise,

fresh sea air, a simple diet, and I could not remain inactive amid the weary throes of the old vessel; she had to be tended, aided, propped. Unguentine's mechanical trees could be death-traps. More than once while raking up the gardens I was caught out there by a wind suddenly rising, momentarily seduced by the clatter of the leaves and padded boughs, until the groan of bending metal would tell me something was going to fall, was falling—but which? Which teetering? Where to run? The huge green claw, hairs of metal hissing, would swoop down past me inches away and strike the earth with a rustling bang, whirrings, a tinkle of bells, with a shower of sparks and a puff of smoke shooting out of the stump at the point where it had rusted through. They always made such a mess. Their white stuffing would waft about the garden for days and days, noxious and impotent pollen. Metal branches that I tripped over and got caught up in like barbed wire. Leaves that would not yellow. The odor of rotting mattresses. One by one they fell down over the years. I managed to cover most of them up by sewing together a dozen trunkloads of old clothes and linen, into huge motley muffs which I draped over them like furniture covers, securing them tightly with cords staked into the ground. Thus they stood or lay and seemed to float about the garden, bloated forms marked with the puzzle-pattern of ancient wardrobes, until my plantings of honeysuckle and wistaria would finally cover them, consume what they could of them; if ever.

Things still grew, except trees, except the livestock which died off, fell overboard, waded or swam away. I didn't mind. It was quieter without them. I had my vegetable patch. Potatoes and yams mainly, a few carrots and greens, a tomato plant or two towards the bow end of the barge, up high on the right in a clear and sunny space with a southern exposure and where, on account of the barge's list, the trees fell the other way. Water I carried in buckets from the stern pump uphill to my vegetables, tasting it each day to make certain it was still fresh. Most things I ate raw, laying out a tablecloth on the ground on the high side of the vegetable patch, with a basin of water, a sharp knife, a plate, a napkin, and I would sit there a while in silence and look over the short rows and tops of green, then wander amongst my plants to pull up a carrot or pick a tomato, return to my spot and wash them, eat them, perhaps return for more. I took my time. They grew slowly, I had no wish to rush them. With dinner I would watch the sun setting through the twisted struts of the dome, stove in here and there and glassless except where beaded gleams of sunlight indicated a sliver still resisting the winds, and all across the marsh long-legged birds would settle in for the night, vanish in the grass; a mist might begin to rise, and off in the distance the hoarse barkings of seals and sea lions, moments when the surf only sighed, not pounded. Perhaps it was they who drove in those tiny fish like sardines which came close to the barge in shallow water, beneath its silvered surface, and bred there before my very eyes, on and on, swarms that came and went. Cold months I sometimes netted up a few and fried them over the fire in the pilot-house, now galley, now bedroom, now my little house with water lapping at the sill since that day when the hull finally gave out and flooded everything below deck.

I remember the evacuation. It took almost a week. In all those years of solitude it was the one time I raised

my voice and called in desperation for Unguentine, to
have his help, his guidance, his ingenuity. Otherwise, I
scarcely missed him. I wanted to recount to him my
adventure in the bilge below the stern deck when I was
wandering around down there to see how all the bulkheads and pipes and machines were doing, all that
ironwork rusting away, neglected, silent, sealed off for so
many years. I was armed with a board on account of my
fear of rats and snakes, and happened to thrust the end
of it against the hull near the old propeller shaft. It went
clear through, to my amazement, and with no more
resistance than a pie-crust. Hastily I withdrew it, expect-
ing to be enveloped in a shower of water or a jumbled
whirlpool, be pursued or floated up the stairs and shot
into the air as the whole barge crumbled into pieces and
sank into the mud and water, leaving me adrift in the
marsh, alone, muddy, clutching at the last debris of
what had been. But no, nothing happened. I bent down
and peered through the hole. The light was dim; I could
see nothing. Finally I dared reach into it and succeeded
in withdrawing a handful of black muck and white
roots, whereupon there began to flow a small trickle of
dank water. I sensed I was about to have a flood on my
hands. Indeed, within minutes it grew into a hardy
spout, belching and erectile, its surging spray spotted
with a multitude of tiny frogs, fish, the bright leaves of
water-cress. I stood on a box, wondered what to do.
There were things to be moved upstairs and above deck.
Which? Which first? Which second? I ran. Most of the
hatchways were rusted and jammed open, and even
those I succeeded in closing in the path of the cheerfully
babbling stream did no good: the bulkheads were
cracked and fissured all over the barge below deck and

the water quickly found the way. But still I could not decide. So I simply moved everything I could carry above deck with the intention of sorting it out later up there, down to a few treasured possessions which I would stow in the skiff and on the swimming platform. It was a frenzied week. Laden down with bundles and boxes, dragging trunks and suitcases behind me, I staggered and crawled up those narrow stairs hundreds of times, day and night, with pots and pans and dishware, sacks of potatoes, bedding, small tables, chairs, box upon box of Unguentine's tools and materials, nautical instruments, ropes, cables; my rugs, my curtains and countless things I knew I could never use but felt compelled to save from those rising waters. And I would have gone on after the water was knee-deep, would even have attempted to learn how to unbolt the cabinets in the galley, dismantle the stove, save an attractive oil-lamp in the old engine-room—had it not been for the rats, flushed out in ever greater numbers from hiding-places I had not known about before, thank God. I gave up, sealed closed the hatchway above the stairs, laid myself down on it and fell immediately into the sleep of utter exhaustion.

I slept perhaps for days. When I awoke and raised my head to find myself surrounded by heaps of household goods and bloated tree tents, a flea-market, a warehouse of damaged goods, a circus in disorder, amid all this unaccountable debris, I could have gone back to sleep and left it at that, finally unaccountable. There had been no beginnings. There would be no end. In this vast rangeland of junk I would awaken now and then, tidy up here and there, make false order, sleep again, wake up anew in another chaos, do my work anew, resume sleep. And when after several weeks it became apparent

96

that the barge had no intention of sinking, or was unable to, was, perhaps, solidly encased in a mud life-preserver a quarter of a mile in diameter, I saw how foolish I had been and realized that the time had come to simplify my life. I had no need of museums, collections, mementoes. So I opened up the hatch to the stairs below deck and into that dark well of sloshing water I threw back all I had dragged upstairs. Grimly at first, calculating my losses, but gradually then with calm, until with joy, until song and liberations, until I filled it all up to the sill and closed the door, shoving the rest into the pond in the cargo hold. I saved only a few kitchen utensils, dishes, some blankets, two changes of clothes and a heavy coat for winter.

Jauntily, suitcase in hand, I walked over to the pilot-house and moved in. It was a small place, nine by six, but ample for my needs. The pilot wheel I succeeded in unscrewing, hung above the window; the other levers and controls I left as they were to drape my clothes over, air the bedding on. A small mattress already lay on a row of footlockers; these I dragged outside and pried open one afternoon: more old clothes, papers, letters I had stored away decades before and which I now shoved overboard with only the briefest of visits from my fingers. There was a small box of photographs all curled up and yellowed, photographs of Unguentine in athletic poses perhaps identical to ones he now held elsewhere— on another barge, with another woman? Of myself embraced by a forgotten landscape, young thing, unknowing, unwise, no doubt peering through time to this moment of being able to gaze back on it all, but still unknowing, unwise, tossing it all over the railing to a shallow splash. They floated on and on, taking days to

97

submerge. Lilies, water faces, friends, family, pets. The mud eventually claimed them. As they silted deeper and deeper in they might fossilize, those faces, to be touched by a germ of life eons hence, to move again, breed again, be photographed again.

Meanwhile years passed. Tired of living under the threat of being brained by a falling strut of the dome, I took an axe to the lower braces and chopped them away at the rate of one a day until after several months, the whole thing gently sagged to earth with a sigh. The wood, being cracked and rotted, was easily broken up into firewood, gave off the rich fragrance of hickory as it burned. I polished the wooden decks once a week, boarded over stretches gnawed away by termites, where water seeped up from the flooded hold. The pilot-house roof leaked in heavy rains; I patched it with sheets of tin salvaged from the shed where I stored the garden tools. I covered the trash in the cargo hold with a foot of earth and planted a few tufts of marsh grass in it. I built a little walkway out of old lumber across to the swimming platform, dug a hole in the mud, lined it with dried grasses and bailed it out again and again until the water finally flowed clear and I could take a daily bath. But now and then I vacationed from it all. I would retire to a quiet spot in the garden and enclose myself in the hammock slung between two mechanical trees that still seemed solid and unrusted in the roots, and hold myself motionless and silent for days and nights on end, breathing no more than a sparrow's ration of air, and just listen, listen to all the sounds. Sometimes I would no longer hear them, only the timeless silences between. It seemed where I stayed for endless years, but then a moment, a minute, a second would flash into time with all the roar and clatter of subways, the awful din of garbage cans being emptied: my own breathing, my heartbeats. It was still going on somewhere. Deep inside. Deep under. However much I might try to shove aside the business of being on two feet, arms swinging around and chattering to grab at something, tear it apart, put it back together, clean it, store it, eat it. Sometimes I would tip myself from the hammock and drop to the ground and lie flat on my stomach upon a dusty patch of earth where I could trace a miniature landscape in the sand and dry grass, there to journey with a purple sow bug across an empty plain, go home, with only a baggage of dust, flecks, scraps. Sometimes I fell upon a traffic of ants or a cluster of bees drinking from a puddle, or a spider come down to ground for some furtive transaction there, my pet populations, true and ultimate heirs: but would they let me join them? Their peace, the soothing silence of things that were only a few inches away, enough distance, too much even by the impossible span of a hand's worth, so impossible to bridge, fling oneself across, little gap, to look.

The ailing barge soon would loudly call again; something would topple over, start leaking, jam up; groan, gurgle, suck. Yearly it settled deeper into the mud until it was almost impossible to tell where barge ended and marsh began, it tilted this way, now that, like a great old bird which had got stuck in its own nest far beyond its time and was now pressed in on all sides by generations of restless descendants. The marsh grass grew higher, thicker; there were clumps of bushes like willows. Once I tested the mud beyond the railings with a long pole and found that beneath the shallow pools of water, beneath the sodden islands of rich green, there were several inches of soft mud, then in places a hard, packed surface which extended beyond the reach of my pole, perhaps even as far as the vanished sea. For one day, and I could not be certain which, it had withdrawn from my view; possibly during those sweltering months of drought when my vegetable patch needed watering dawn to dusk and when I had spent whole days doing nothing but throwing the empty bucket over the rail, dipping up a scanty ration of water, carrying it uphill, pouring it into the rows and basins of earth, watching it sink so fast into the crusted dryness. My lettuce bolted, went to seed; also I ran out of carrots. But during that time I remember looking out to sea once with the field-glasses in the hope of sighting a mass of thunderheads peeping over the horizon, for the promise of water, a showerbath in the rain, but seeing none; remarking however that the distant green-and-blue ribbons of sea seemed to be spotted with grassy pads of mud like that which grew around the barge, the sudden absence of surf, the white lines, the bursts of spray. I swore I still heard it from somewhere out there, but with so many years at sea my ears would be forever filled with its reverberations; in similar manner my habit of not gazing beyond the railings of the barge those years, what with the mass of finely etched seascapes already crowding my brain, their lines fixed and precise, symmetrical, needing no corrections, no additions: I pulled them down like blinds while tending the earth and garden, not wanting to lift my head. When I next looked up, climbing even to the high side of the barge to have a better view, the sea was gone. There were only spots of blue here and there in the distance, on all horizons, as if the barge had been transported some recent night to a pampas land, rich and fertile, or to fields of sugar cane. I drew breath in sharply through my nostrils. I knew the smell. I still remembered it. Once while out in the middle of a desolate sea with lukewarm waters, in a strong wind, that scent had torn through me with such speed and violence that I collapsed to the deck and sobbed; now embraced by it on all sides, I strolled down the little hill and into the gardens, noted a few holes in the tree covers, and wondered: what would it be like to live without the presence of the sea?

I was to know soon enough. I had to weave old branches and dry reeds into the fixtures of the railing, into a fence to discourage wildlife from poaching away my meagre garden, creatures I never saw but began to hear with increasing frequency. There were those soft squeaking noises from out in the marsh, perhaps only the blades of grass rubbing together, or water dripping in some odd way, or things growing and toppling over. One night I thought I heard a dog barking out there. Another I lay sleepless in the pilot-house, axe in hand, terrorized by the sucking footsteps of a heavy beast which seemed stuck in the mud, which whined and grunted all night long. Next day I found my bathing hole next to the swimming platform befouled by a pair of speckled turds, had to dig a new one. The marsh grass grew higher, well over my head, and once a week I trimmed it back away from the railing, using the stalks to reinforce my fence. I nailed some old boards together into a gate so I could close off the path to the swimming platform at night, hung it with a bell. At times, when looking out over the profusion of growth in the endless marsh, I could not help but remember the first years of the barge when the gardens had been like that, almost impenetrable from one end to the other, and perhaps this too, this land, this shimmering green was somehow being cultivated. Through field-glasses I saw dark masses of green off in the far distance, like ranks of trees. I saw spots of orange and red, like fruit, like flowers; there were pollens in the air, I found handfuls of tiny seeds in nooks and crannies in the pilot-house, in protected corners of the garden where winds had driven them. One day I was startled by the sound of ripping cloth from the tent over the fallen Chestnut Anna and looked up to see a flash of living leaves as a young poplar burst through the rotting cloth near the embrace of one of my old bathrobes and a pair of Unguentine's overalls. We stared at each other a few minutes, warily. Then I reached up and ripped away some of the cloth, straightened its branches all bent and crooked from the months of confinement.

As resuscitated by the pressures of teeming growth beyond my fence, the gardens revived. I let things grow where they would, how they would, keeping only the vegetable patch weeded, encouraging only a small tree which might some day produce a few fruit, clearing only my pathways from stem to stern and the ambleway up the hill to my belvedere. It was a happy time. While my brain churned with old nautical terms I had long refused to learn and now had no use for, port, starboard, knots and all the speeds ahead and fore and aft, azimuths and pole stars, another part of me awaited dreamily some easy moment when the growth on the barge might reach a vigor and density such that I would be confined to a small green cage, me with my pruning shears all dulled and rusted away and with nothing to do but curl up and find an endless sleep. But my reveries, my

102

simple life soon fell under new harassments. For months I tried to ignore them. When finally I caught a cold, the first in over thirty years, I knew my solitude was at an end. To absentmindedness I had attributed a blank piece of paper tacked to the pilot-house door, that I had put it up one day intending to scrawl some reminder to myself, had forgotten, had rediscovered it next day electrified at the thought that it might be another's handiwork, had twirled around to stare at the blank green wall of vegetation that stood beyond my fence. I had taken it down, tossed it overboard. There were other signs. Weeds and brush began to vanish from the spot in the center of the barge where once the lawn had stood. I found a neat row of petunias, already beginning to bloom, lining one of my pathways. My tree tents became like greenhouses, another one ripping open every day or so under the thrust of a new growth of saplings. I began to lie in wait. By night I hid in thickets armed with field-glasses and axe, seeking to surprise the intruder and order him off the premises; perhaps it was a farmer sprung suddenly out of the mud to become a neighbour attempting to annex my modest plot by performing nocturnal improvements, intending some day to slap me with a claim. Boundaries? Property lines? Easements? Rights of way? I struggled in my mind to remember how they worked, wondered what to do; even, how to do anything at all. These ten years alone in my hermitage had put me out of speech; I was no longer young, my charms were all silted over, my wardrobe rotted, the silver service leaked, the cups had long since been broken and I had gone to eating off broad leaves, drank tea from an old bottle.

I set up snares one night, a tripwire that crossed the

pathways several places in the garden and along the fence so that anyone climbing inside would set the bell on the gate to clanging; next night indeed it clanged, and I heard footsteps running, I heard the crack of branches from my perch atop the pilot-house roof, but saw nothing in the dark. Unguentine, I wondered, clumsy as ever? Come back after a decade away to trouble me with new beginnings? Not long after as my nights grew wary and sleepless, my days a struggle to keep alert, I began to hear the sounds I knew were his coming from out in the marsh, his squeaks, that obscene whistling noise, the humming that sometimes went on for hours. How could I turn a deaf ear? For with them time began to flow again, to wash back over all that had been, to revivify now, to sweep before my eyes old flotsam, old jetsam, old tears that I thought had gone forever from a worn-out memory. Beautiful as it all might have been, once had been enough. Please, not again. But he knew when I slept. One morning I awoke to find a pot of freshly cut daisies on my doorstep; I left them to wilt and die there. Several days later he replaced them. I threw them overboard. Eventually, ten yards beyond my fence and far beyond my reach, he erected a sort of stand like a bird-feeding tray, wired a pot on top of it in such a way that I might not knock it off with a well-heaved dirt clod; daily then the daisies appeared up there, were daily renewed.

His courtship was persistent, even obscene. From my lookouts on the hill and atop the pilot-house I could see in the distance the cane-breaks quiver as he moved about, sometimes spending a whole day circling the barge though never permitting me to have a glimpse of him. Once he wove a great phallus out of sticks and vines, thrust it up through the grass and proceeded to parade it around the barge until sunset. Thus another sleepless night. I grew tired and fell ill. I could see his strategy: bedridden and driven to despair, I would cry for his help. Quickly, with what strength I had left, I harvested all the vegetables that were ripe and would keep, filled the pilot-house with baskets of potatoes, onions, squash and a dozen jugs of water, a small bundle of firewood, and locked the door and pulled the curtains closed. It would be my last and final retreat. I had already lived too long as it was. If he wished, he could take over the rest of the barge so long as he left me in peace. He could even repair the hull and dredge the mud from the hold and dig a channel-way to the sea and set sail again for all I cared, and as my fever rose and I lay back upon the hard mattress and closed my eyes, I knew I would even resist his whisperings under the door, his notes, his glossy descriptions of fantastic seascapes, of waves, of seagulls perching expectant on the railings, the sound of the wind through the trees and flapping sails, I would plug my ears up, not listen, not hear. Yet my resolve wavered now and then. Before nightfall, my temperature dropping a degree or two, I would eat some carrots, sip water, then draw myself to my feet and unsteadily part the curtains a fraction of an inch, peep out. Nothing changed. He was never to be seen out there. Silently each day the chamber-pot I slipped out of the door, my mortalities within, vanished to be returned cleaned and empty. I became bored. I ate too much, grew fat, grasped at the baskets of food he took to leaving outside the door when he had guessed the supply inside was running low. Months passed. It all seemed too familiar. He had trapped me again, or finally, or needlessly into putrefying, bloated and perspiring, in this cramped and angular space; he must have known and calculated that my years of solitude had fortified my will to the degree that I would never again expose my shame to him, never ask his mercy. I stopped eating, drank only a few cups of water a day. I withdrew my hands from my body, would not touch it, would not look down at it in the semi-darkness. All my organs seemed in revolt. They shoved and kicked, swelled and deflated. I submitted to fantasies to pregnancy, some comfort in my lethargy and waiting, of an elderly child-birth upon one of Unguentine's old sperm which till now had lain dormant within my body like a grain entombed, to burst into germination long after all the walls had fallen. And when the pains finally grew sharp I thought that death should come like that—like childbirth, into the birth of silence and no light—and I stood up one last time and pushed the curtains apart to have a glimpse across the gardens, my fence, to the waves upon waves of velvet green beyond. I fell, then. Someone screamed, I heard sobs, I heard coughing; suddenly I wanted to sleep. But the light from the window was too bright. When I raised my head from the floor, my mouth agape and some strange noise lowly pouring from it, I looked across my huge stomach heaving with contractions and thought to see Unguentine flow slowly out from between my legs and crowd my knees, or a somewhat dwarfish version of him, yet with the white beard, the flowing white hair. He was crouching now, I saw his eyes blink and open, I saw a smile flash across his damp face the instant before his features went rigid and he toppled over backwards with a heavy thud. I could no longer raise my head, see where he was; yet I knew now he had

106

come back to me at last only to die, was dead, to smile only, no more. A rivulet of my blood was soon flowing across the floor in pursuit of him. Soon myself, my body. Thus I joined him.

1972 was a difficult year for the novel. This might—and perhaps should—be said of all years and times, since the novel is forever, genetically, finding everything a struggle and all things difficult (I think we're supposed to be worried when the novel does not do this). But 1972 was particularly special in its overshadowing, domineering, *mattering* way. It was a year that refused to cede an inch to the make-believe. The merely imaginary might finally have seemed trifling up against some of the defining and grisly moments of the century that collided that year and chewed up every available dose of attention in the culture. 1972, in short, produced the Watergate scandal, the Munich Massacre, and Bloody Sunday. Nixon traveled to China in 1972, and the last U.S. troops finally departed Vietnam. It wasn't clear that a novel had leverage against all of this atrocity, deceit, transgression, and milestone, let alone a novel posing as a ship's log, narrated by a widowed ship slave who has witnessed logic-defying architecture, radical ecological invention, and faked a pregnancy while being banished—by her alcoholic, abusive husband—from all land and humanity.

Forget that painting (or sculpture, or the better poetry) was never asked to compete with the news, or to be the news. The novel's weird burden of relevance—to reflect and anticipate the times, to grab headlines, to be somehow current, while not also disgracing the language—was being shirked all over the place, and Stanley Crawford, already unusually capable of uncoiling his brain and repacking it in his head in a new, gnarled design for every book he wrote, was chief among those writers who seemed siloed in a special, ahistorical field, working with private alchemical tools, producing work just out of tune enough to disrupt the flight of the birds that passed his hideout.

Architectural dreamwork, end-times seascapes so barren they seem cut from the pages of the Bible, coolly-rendered Rube Goldberg apparati, and the crushing sadness that results when you tie your emotional fortunes to a person whose tongue is so fat in his mouth he can barely speak, mark this little masterpiece of a novel. Cast as a soliloquy in the form of a ship's log, a grief report from someone who has no good insurance she will ever be heard, the novel moves fluidly between its major forms: love song, a treatise on gardening at sea, an argument against the company of others, and a dark science expo for exquisite inventions like a hybrid lichen that makes things invisible. Published by Alfred A. Knopf under the editorial guidance of Gordon Lish, the fiction world's singular Quixote—a champion of innovative styles and formal ambition—there may have been no better year in which to tuck such an odd, exquisite book. Instead of rushing for relevance and breaking the news, Crawford was taking the oldest news of all—it is strange and alone here, even when we are surrounded by people, and there is a great degree of pain to be felt—and reporting it as nautical confessional. The result, now thirty-six years later, seems to prove that interior news, the news of what it feels like to want too much from another person, will not readily smother under archival dust.

To be sure, Crawford's focus in *Log*—the special toxins that steam off of a marriage—was happily at-large in the literary work of his peers (possibly so much at-large that its shadow is still staining the ground on which we walk), but while most of Crawford's contemporaries were staging their loveless, white-knuckle relationship fiction in a spume of alcohol, boxed up in fresh suburban sheet rock, Crawford put his unhappily married couple, the Unguentines, to sea, rendered them as solitary (if not so innocent) as Adam and Eve, and he cursed them to be so awkwardly fit for human behavior that every kind of congress had to be reinvented and mythologized anew. If *The Mrs Unguentine* is so large and equipped it seems more like an island, it is also a floating stage for human experimentation, beyond the strictures of society, and the novel itself is a playbook for rethinking just what two people are supposed to do together when most of the livable world is out of reach. And to make their dilemma special, so we could see the nosedive of the Unguentines' failed love through a crystal lens that Crawford ground himself from his own blend, he canopied the bad marriage with a fantastical dome, a literary invention so beautiful it doesn't hog the spotlight so much as become a kind of distorted monocle through which to see this experiment in isolation, gardening, and love go terribly, terribly wrong.

This may have been the first time that readers could sample a collision of such radically different literary sensibilities as Ingmar Bergman and Jules Verne: the bleak, life-loathing (affirming, loathing, affirming, who knows anymore) sensibility of the great artist of domestic cruelty, Bergman, with the wondrous vision and spectacle of Verne, the adventure story mad scientist. Call it Scenes from a Marriage on a Mysterious Island, because *The Mrs Unguentine* is more landmass than boat, a garden of Eden with very little joy and not one dose of shame, where the only solution to the endless pain of love is to hurl oneself overboard, which Mr. Unguentine does, only to keep courting his woman from the deeps, or from the dead, it isn't really clear. Faking his own death just to reset the romance and return to courting? Colossally cruel or intensely romantic, or maybe both? This was the highest drama, a marriage on the rocks set in the weird colors of, if not science fiction, then really strange fiction that hews as much to ship design and greenhouse invention as it does to characters. The aloof approach to the sanctity of marriage, what indeed at times can seem like a satire of bad marriage fiction (she wants to talk, he wants to work and be alone, she wants kids, he drinks, he hits, she lies, he disappears), lulls us into susceptibility for the deep magic that occurs on this boat, and it would prove to be Stanley Crawford's perfect art in later books to stage his deeply human stories—stories about the failure to love properly or deeply or at all—in bizarre, defended, solipsistic worlds.

Crawford's description of the dome, secreted into the text with bored, offhand logic, introduces a theme that would later become a long-standing obsession (in such books as *Some Instructions* [1978] and *Petroleum Man* [2005]): patriarchs who cruelly show their love through radical inventions and the construction of ingenious, if useless, systems. If these men cannot much speak or love or hug, if they can't be basically kind and open and interested, they can impart information, a syllabus wrenched from an arcane mind, with the hopes that it will be received as the ultimate loving gift. As much as we hear of Mr. Unguentine's failure at human interaction, the entire ship's design seems somehow his best act of love. Every bit of rigging and composting is a shrine. He will take his wife away to sea and never explain why, or even speak. He will fashion a secret identity for himself that brooks no interruption or interrogation. But in return he will build her a more fascinating world than any she could expect on land, even while depriving her of the basic things she wants. It's a complicated way to show love, full of spectacle, vain performance, and ego. The irony is so entirely *not* lost on Mrs. Ungentine that she's crushed by it.

In Crawford's memoir of farming, *A Garlic Testament* (1992), he remarks of himself that, as a young man, he "developed a craving for what I called the real." It is his pursuit of this goal, in a body of work that is as rigorously inventive as it is obsessed with the human tragedy, that has marked him as a writer attuned to the most potent, and timeless, possibilities in literary fiction.

BEN MARCUS, 2008

SELECTED DALKEY ARCHIVE PAPERBACKS

www.dalkeyarchive.com

SELECTED DALKEY ARCHIVE PAPERBACKS

FOR A FULL LIST OF PUBLICATIONS, VISIT:
www.dalkeyarchive.com